W.W. MITCHELL

Cataclysm Kin

At the core of every tale lies a dream worth pursuing, a narrative worth crafting. My beloved children, you are the reason I write. Without your radiant smiles, your joyous laughter, and the boundless love you share, my stories—this one and all the others—would simply not exist. You are my everything, my entire universe.

Contents

Preface

If you're reading this, I can only assume you're smart enough not to get confused. Then again, there's a lot to take in. Welcome to the beginning of a very big, very complicated world. It's one that will challenge your perceptions, twist your expectations, and maybe even have you questioning your own reality. But that's the fun of it, right?

There are plenty of terms to remember, so—because I'm such a kind and thoughtful author—I've included a glossary. It would've been downright cruel to let you wander blind through all the lingo, and I'm far too generous for that. You'll need it. And don't be shy—refer back to it as much as you like. It's there for you, your trusty guide through this labyrinth.

The way the characters talk? Yeah, it gets weird. The things they reference? Even weirder. But don't worry—you've got this. Probably. You might feel lost a few times, but that's part of the ride. Just lean into the chaos, and soon enough, it'll start making sense—or at least you'll get used to the weirdness.

You might even find yourself speaking this strange new dialect in your sleep. Stranger things have happened.

And as you dive deeper into the story, remember one thing: nothing here is as it seems. The lines between good and bad, right and wrong, are often blurred, twisted, and sometimes nonexistent. So, try not to judge too quickly. Keep your wits about you, and whatever you do, don't skip the glossary. Trust me, you'll thank me later.

Enjoy the glossary. Try not to get lost. And above all, keep an open mind. You're about to embark on something unforgettable.

Realms & Locations

- **Par** — A once-glorious celestial realm, home to the divine race known as the Par. Now a broken kingdom, its ruins haunted by the consequences of war and betrayal.
- **Kelxsiar Prison** — A subterranean hell beneath Par's ruins, designed to contain corrupted or dangerous beings.
- **Voidspire Engines** — Ancient devices built by the Par to travel between realms. Many now lie shattered and dead, but a few still whisper the secrets of survival.

- **Firmament Temple** — A desecrated temple once sacred to the Par, now a corpse of its former self, watched over by mechanical monstrosities.
- **Vast Sea** — A mythical afterlife believed by the Par to be the ultimate reward—an endless sea where the worthy find peace after death.

Species

- **Par** — A divine race of radiant beings, winged and powerful. Once the architects of great civilizations, now a dying breed scattered across broken worlds.
- **Kelxsiar** — Nightmarish, insectile creatures born of void and cruelty. They are jailers, torturers, and soldiers who infest Par's ruins and hunt survivors.
- **Halphobs** — Ethereal beings of peace, woven from light and organic circuitry. Enslaved by the Kelxsiar despite their wisdom and passive nature.
- **Nerl** — A near-extinct species seen as cursed by Par society. Their blood and lineage carry ancient significance, and their survival poses threats—and hopes—few understand.

- **M.E.P.S. Mutagen** — A corrupting force that infected Kore at birth, altering her physiology into something darker, more dangerous, and impossible to undo.
- **Voidspire Engines** — (also listed under Locations) Instruments of interdimensional travel, forged by the Par with lost technologies that could traverse realities.
- **Kelxsiar Rovers** — Biomechanical monstrosities that patrol and guard ruined areas, part flesh, part machine, driven by the will of the Kelxsiar hive.

Organizations

- **W.A.S.P. (Worldwide Alien and Superhuman Protocol)** — A secretive Earth-based organization that monitors and intervenes in extraterrestrial and superhuman phenomena. Ruthless when necessary.
- **Hunter Sentries** — Units created by the Par to contain threats within their society, often used to imprison or control "tainted" bloodlines.

- **Kin** — In the context of the story, refers both to literal family ties and the deeper, often tragic, bonds between those of Par blood.
- **Vast Sea** — (important enough to repeat) The ultimate afterlife belief among the Par—a place of eternal peace reserved for the honored dead.
- **Sacred Wards** — Seals and glyphs of ancient Par design, used to imprison or bind entities of overwhelming power.
- **Blood Registry** — A scroll recording the noble bloodlines of the Par race. Ominously, not everyone expected appears on it.
- **Mutagenic Curse** — The genetic and spiritual blight caused by exposure to forbidden energies like the M.E.P.S. mutagen.

Acknowledgments

To my beloved wife, whose unwavering commitment to reading and appreciating my work inspires me daily. You are a steadfast reminder to hold onto my dreams. Your support has been invaluable, from my days in a shelter to now, as I stand stronger and wiser. Thank you.

Mom and Dad, your wisdom, guidance, and unwavering support have inspired my creativity to reach new heights.

Dear Colleagues, Friends, and Family, your unwavering support is truly remarkable. It empowers me to reach heights I never thought possible. I am deeply grateful to each of you. This is a heartfelt thank you, dedicated to you.

Prologue

Ara stood motionless, her small body trembling as her golden eyes lingered on the grotesque form of her baby sister.

Kore lay on the cot, her frail frame convulsing slightly beneath the sterile glow of their war-torn dwelling. The air reeked of blood, sweat, and something sour—something unnatural. Their father, the mighty Warlord Farook, loomed nearby. His chiseled face was etched with disgust as he studied the infant before him.

Kore's yellow eyes glowed faintly—unnerving in their brightness. The veins beneath her crimson skin pulsed like living wires. Her tiny fingers curled and stretched, revealing claws that gleamed like polished obsidian. Soft, horned nubs coiled just above her temples, curling ever so slightly with each breath.

"It is an abomination," Farook declared, his voice cracking beneath the weight of his revulsion. "She's infected."

The home technician, a wiry man with eyes too

wide and hands that twitched, shifted uncomfortably. He avoided the Warlord's gaze, locking his attention on the monitor displaying Kore's vitals. "It's exactly as we feared. Kore's anatomy has been corrupted by the M.E.P.S. mutagen. It's… irreversible."

Liava, the girls' mother, stood stiff as stone. Her expression teetered between horror and contempt as she clutched Ara close, shielding the golden-skinned daughter from the sight of her corrupted sibling. Ara, only two years old, was the image of celestial perfection—her luminous complexion gleamed under the flickering light, and the delicate beginnings of white feathers peeked from her back. She was the daughter of promise, a symbol of their species' purity.

"What's wrong with my sister?" Ara's tiny voice broke the oppressive silence, her golden curls framing a face too innocent to understand the weight of the moment.

Farook knelt beside his eldest daughter, his tone softening just slightly. "I'm afraid she'll never grow her wings, Ara. She is… broken."

The finality of his words gripped Ara's chest, though she could not grasp why it hurt so deeply.

Liava's gaze flicked toward the technician. "Is it… contagious?" she asked coldly.

The man hesitated, his discomfort thick in the

air. "We don't believe so. But the safest course of action would be to remove her from the home."

The implication landed with brutal clarity. Farook's jaw tightened. His gaze snapped to Liava—who averted her eyes.

Without a word, Liava handed the screaming infant to the technician. He recoiled slightly before forcing himself to take the child. Kore's wails pierced the room—raw and unrelenting—as if she already understood the betrayal.

"What will become of her?" Farook's voice was hollow, already knowing the answer.

"She'll be raised in containment," the technician replied, placing Kore into a containment tank lined with cold wiring that slithered across her tiny limbs. "Perhaps with the hunter sentries. She could be… useful. A herder, perhaps." His tone was clinical, detached—like Kore was a malfunctioning prototype rather than a child. "There hasn't been a mutagenic child in nearly two hundred revolutions."

Ara's heart ached as she watched Kore disappear into the tank, her cries now muffled by thick glass. For years, Ara would stare at the fenced enclosure where her sister was kept—a prisoner in their own home—and wonder what crime an infant could commit to deserve such punishment.

At ten years old, Ara stood on the edge of the yard, her gaze locked on Kore's cubicle.

Her sister sat cross-legged inside, her claws lazily carving aimless patterns into the steel floor. Kore's yellow eyes had darkened over the years, now swirling with stormy shadows trapped behind glass. Her horns had sharpened, her teeth grown more feral—but her voice, when she spoke, remained hauntingly human.

"Why can't my sister be with us?" Ara asked, her voice trembling with a mix of defiance and desperation.

Farook adjusted the heavy armor draped across his shoulders. His massive axe rested against his side, but he didn't meet her gaze. "She's poisoned. We are fighting a war to keep our realm alive. She is a threat to that survival."

"She's my sister," Ara whispered, but the words caught in her throat like embers.

The Warlord finally turned, his expression a mask of iron. "My daughter grows wings," he said flatly. His eyes flicked toward Kore's cell—then he walked away, armor clanking with each resolute step.

* * *

The Par army marched through the darkness of the new realm, their glowing hands lighting the void ahead. Farook led them, unshaken in posture, but the air thickened with each step. The very ground beneath them seemed to shift and breathe—alive and wrong.

"Warlord… this is not what was briefed," a soldier muttered, unease thick in his voice.

Before Farook could respond, a blade of pure shadow erupted from the dark, piercing his chest. Golden blood sprayed into the air, shimmering like liquid sunlight before splattering across the stone.

The soldiers froze. Horror rippled through the ranks as grotesque silhouettes emerged—Kelxsiar. Cloaked in smoke, their limbs elongated and grotesque, their weapons carved from nightmare.

They tore through the Par like silk—silent, swift, and merciless.

Farook collapsed to his knees, his vision fading. In his final breath, he saw not triumph—but utter annihilation.

* * *

Back at the compound, Ara screamed.

Rifts split the sky, tearing the very fabric of their reality. Kelxsiar spilled into the yard—dozens of them—wearing Par armor like trophies, their black tongues flicking hungrily as they scanned the area.

Their leader emerged—towering, twisted, a mass of sinew and shadow.

He approached Kore's kennel. His voice, deep and guttural, rumbled from within his chest. "You show no fear."

Kore rose, her clawed hands gripping the bars. "What have I to fear?" she said, steady. "You've taken everything."

The creature chuckled darkly. "Then let us test your resolve."

With a click of his tongue, the Kelxsiar dragged Ara and Liava into the yard.

The leader pressed a blade of shadow to Liava's throat. His eyes locked on Kore.

"Do you fear now?" he asked, his voice soaked in malice.

Kore didn't blink. "She is no mother to me. Do it."

The leader hesitated—confusion flickering across his monstrous face.

Kore stepped forward, her yellow eyes glowing like fire through the darkness.

"Do it," she spat. "Prove to me you're not as weak as they were."

The blade trembled in his grasp.

And then it moved—

I

The Demon of Par

"I am that which they feared, and that which their minds could not fathom. In sooth, my heart was ne'er fashioned to tread the path my father laid. He did cast me from his bloodline—as one casts a stone into the abyss—and in so doing, did stir a fury deep within the blackened pit of my soul. My cause was not born of duty to kin, nor for a name long dead... but for mine own becoming. For something unmade. I am... Kore."

1

"Thy Witches We Be Not"

The evening air hung heavy with a foreboding stillness—the kind that pricked at the edges of awareness and made shadows seem alive. Bethany stood poised at the window of their weathered cabin, her fingers brushing aside the gossamer curtain as she peered into the void of night. The dirt path beyond was barren, lifeless, but her gaze remained sharp and unrelenting, as though the darkness itself might conspire against them.

The wind whispered faintly, carrying with it the scent of damp earth and faint traces of ash—a bitter reminder of the Salem fires, where fear had burned brighter than reason.

"Bethany," came Edith's hushed voice from across the room, taut with unease, "are we alone?"

Her words lingered like a fragile prayer, an attempt to will safety into existence.

Bethany turned her head slightly, her expression resolute but shadowed by doubt. "Not a soul stirs," she replied, her voice low yet tinged with defiance. "Yet why must we continue to cower like hunted beasts?"

"Thou dost know the reason well," Edith said, her tone sharpened by strain. "This world is neither prepared nor willing to comprehend beings such as we."

Bethany exhaled sharply, frustration clinging to the sound as her fingers tightened around the curtain's edge. "And why should I care for the readiness of men? I do not mourn their ignorance, nor will I endure this perpetual flight in silence."

"A celestial ascent does not pass unseen," Edith warned, quieter now, yet her words cut deep. "Do not think for a moment that the eyes of this realm are blind to thy actions."

Their shared cabin, though humble, had become a fragile sanctuary—a reprieve from the hysteria sweeping Salem like plague. Superstition hung thick in the air; every flickering candle and whispered tale was scrutinized for its alignment with witchcraft. Even here, safety felt as transient as breath on glass.

Then—movement. A distant murmur rising from the forest edge. At first, a tremor. Then, the sound swelled—shouts, footsteps, the unmistakable clamor of a mob.

Bethany stiffened. Her golden eyes narrowed as torchlight flickered into view—orange flames dancing like predator eyes in the dark.

"Burn the witches!"

The chant emerged as a guttural rumble, then swelled into a cacophony of rage. Voices thick with venom filled the night with violent purpose.

Bethany's lips curled into a grimace. "It appears thy warnings were in vain. They come for us regardless."

Edith's face paled. Her hands trembled as she clutched her shawl tighter. "Bethany, please! We must make them see reason!"

Bethany's gaze darkened, her resolve hardening. "Reason? What reason can be found in the mind of a rabid beast?"

The mob drew closer. Faces twisted with zeal. Pitchforks. Axes. Firelight reflecting in their eyes. At their head, a burly man in a crooked hat raised his torch.

"Come forth, Bethany Guzman and Edith Guzman!" he bellowed. "Thou art accused of witchcraft and consorting with the Devil!"

Bethany stepped into the doorway, chin high. "Thou art mistaken. We are no witches."

"Silence!" the man roared, met with a chorus of agreement. "Thy lies shall not save thee!"

"I caution thee against this folly," Bethany said, her voice a dagger cloaked in calm. "Turn away, and thou may yet live to see another dawn."

"Thy arrogance damns thee!" a townsman shouted. "We have seen thy sister take flight—proof of her infernal nature!"

Edith's voice rang out, urgent. "We bear no ill will! I beseech thee, do not succumb to lies!"

But the crowd surged. The cabin door shattered. Chaos.

A torchman lunged toward Bethany.

"Wilt thou burn me with that flame, good sir?" she asked, low and steady.

"I shall burn this cursed dwelling to ash!"

Bethany's expression twisted—golden eyes flaring crimson. A light spilled from her like a bleeding wound. Her voice dropped into something no longer mortal.

"Thou shouldst have heeded my warning."

"Bethany, no!" Edith cried.

But it was too late.

Horns erupted from Bethany's brow. Obsidian. Gleaming. Her wings unfurled with a sickening snap—leathery, wide, monstrous. Her fangs elongated. A growl escaped her lips, deep and unholy.

The mob recoiled.

Bethany became fury incarnate. Her foot collided with a man's chest, sending him flying through the wall. Another fell to her claws. Fire spilled across the rug.

"Enough, Bethany!" Edith screamed, tears streaming. "Cease this madness!"

"Madness?" Bethany snarled. "This is justice! Remember thy place—and who it was that saved thy wretched life!"

* * *

PAR

Ara and Kore are barely more than whispers in the void. Fugitive daughters of a dying realm—bound by cursed blood and tethered by desperation. Between them lies a Voidspire Engine—an artifact stitched together from the dead science of negative matter.

It pulses—alive. Their only hope.

They're running from Par, a world built on suffering. A place where the Kelxsiar ruled without mercy, and where Kore was turned into a monster. Forced to hunt her own, drink rusted water, eat scraps of filth, and bleed for their entertainment.

And yet—she's still standing.

Ara bursts into the chamber, breathless and

shaking, weaving through corridors slick with shadow and pain.

"Sister," she says, clutching the rusted bars of Kore's cage, "it's me."

Kore stirs. Her eyes are pitch black. Talons curl against the floor.

"You're not my sister."

"I never abandoned you. I never even got the chance to know you. I'm here now—to make that right."

Kore scoffs, her fanged grin jagged and cruel. "You think you know me? What do you see when you look at me?"

"I see my equal. I see my blood."

Silence hangs between them. A tremor runs through Kore's fingers.

Ara steps closer. "You were wronged—not by me, but by them."

Kore's breath is shallow. "Run, Ara. The Kelxsiar will kill you before you take your next breath."

"I'm not leaving without you."

Ara's hands flare with golden light. The rusted bars melt, dripping molten steel onto the floor. Kore watches.

She's free.

For the first time—truly free.

"Where would we even go?" Kore asks.

"I found a Voidspire Engine," Ara says. "It still

works. It can get us out."

Kore stiffens. No lies. No hesitation. Just truth.

"And this realm?" she mutters, but she already knows the answer. Their people turned their backs on her. Their parents—her own father—called her an abomination.

Ara's voice is steady. "You're all I have left."

"Father was wrong."

And something in Kore shifts.

"If your wings never come back," Ara whispers, "then I'll carry you."

And for the first time, Kore lets herself believe.

But freedom is never given—it is taken.

* * *

The Voidspire Engine looms in the shadows like a monolithic grave marker, its unnatural glow pulsing with eerie, living veins of light. The deep, thrumming hum vibrates through their bones—it feels sentient, aware.

Ara lays a hand upon its surface. "This is our way out."

Kore only nods. The weight of this moment sits heavy upon them both. For the first time, they are choosing their fate.

The air thickens. A cold, predatory stillness slithers into the chamber.

They are being hunted.

A chill runs through Kore's spine. She knows this presence.

"It is here." Kore breathes.

Ara's fingers twitch. "What is it?"

Kore's blackened eyes narrow. "A hunter."

The lights of the Engine stutter, flickering erratically—plunging the chamber into flashes of light and suffocating darkness. A growl slithers from the abyss, low and guttural, reverberating through the walls.

Kore tenses, claws flexing.

Then—the beast strikes.

A sinuous appendage lashes from the shadows, wrapping around Ara's leg, YANKING her violently into the air.

She screams—the sound of flesh meeting cold steel echoes as she slams into the wall. A crack. A sickening snap.

Kore lunges. Her claws dig deep into the creature's writhing mass. Green, acidic blood erupts from the wound, sizzling against her skin.

The beast snarls—its flickering form finally revealing itself in the dim, a nightmare of jagged flesh and shifting void. Its head—if it could be called such—splits open, a jagged maw lined with rows of twisted, mismatched teeth. Its sockets drip black mist, leaking from nothingness.

Ara chokes out a cry, clutching her arm—her bones are broken.

Kore's fury ignites.

"RUN!" she bellows, her voice no longer human. It is raw. It is monstrous.

Ara shakes her head, defiant even in pain. "Not without thee!"

Her wings ignite, exploding in brilliant golden light. The chamber is bathed in celestial fire.

She snatches Kore, wrapping her in a protective embrace. They surge forward, diving toward the Engine.

The beast shrieks—a sound that is not of this world, a sound that frays the very fabric of existence.

The sisters crash through the gate, hurtling into the void beyond.

* * *

The flames consumed the cabin with ravenous hunger, the inferno roaring like a living beast as the roof collapsed in a fiery cascade. Embers danced violently against the night, their flickering light casting grotesque shadows upon the surrounding woods. Smoke curled skyward, thick and black, staining the heavens with its reach.

Through the chaos, Bethany burst forth, her wings tearing through the choking haze. The leathery expanse of her bat-like appendages glinted in the firelight, an ominous silhouette against the raging storm of embers. She ascended with an effortless grace, her form cutting through the heat and smoke as if she thrived in their destructive embrace. Below, the terrified cries of the retreating townsfolk faded into irrelevance, drowned by the crackle of the consuming fire.

Edith lingered at the threshold of the crumbling inferno, her eyes fixed on the fleeing mob. Her breath caught as she felt the weight of their hatred, but her hesitation lasted only a heartbeat. With a grim resolve, she stepped forward, the flames casting eerie highlights across her pale face. Her wings erupted from her back with a deafening tear, their white feathers shimmering with an ethereal glow. The sudden burst of light pierced the smoke, a beacon amidst the chaos, and she soared heavenward, leaving the fiery wreckage behind.

Bethany was already high above, her movements swift and unrelenting. The cold air bit at her skin as she climbed higher, the searing heat below growing faint. Her lips curled into a smirk as she heard

Edith's distant voice pierce the air.

"Beth! Halt thy course!" Edith's cry carried desperation, but Bethany answered only with a derisive laugh that echoed across the burning landscape.

Edith's wings beat furiously as she pursued, the soft hum of her flight lost to the crackle of fire and the night's howling wind. "Hold, sister!" she called again, her voice stern yet pleading.

Bethany glanced back, her eyes blazing crimson. "Keep pace, if thou art able! Mayhap our next refuge should be to thine liking—someplace exotic, perchance?" Her words were sharp and mocking, dripping with venomous amusement.

"Enough of thy insolence!" Edith roared, her voice cutting through the tumult like a blade. She surged forward, her fingers outstretched, and grasped Bethany's wing with firm defiance.

The contact ignited a maelstrom of fury in Bethany. She wheeled around with a snarl, her fangs elongating into razor-sharp points. Her gaze burned like molten fire as she hissed, "Thou darest to lay hands upon me?"

"Thou hast overstepped thy bounds!" Edith retorted, her voice trembling with righteous indignation.

Bethany's lips curled into a sneer. "And what wouldst thou do, dear sister? Smite me with thy divine hand? Bind me with thy sanctimonious chains?"

Edith's jaw tightened, her voice steady as she declared, "If thou continuest to defile the mortal realm, I shall do what I must. Even if it means casting thee into the abyss."

Bethany laughed, the sound low and menacing, sending shivers through the night air. "Then come, sister. Try thy best."

Edith's hands ignited with a celestial flame, its golden light a stark contrast to the darkness that clung to Bethany like a second skin. The two hovered high above the earth, the wind whipping between them as the tension mounted.

"Very well," Edith said, her voice an unyielding vow. "If thou wilt not cease, I shall cast thee back into the inferno from which thou hast risen." She reached for Bethany, her hand alight with holy fire.

Bethany swatted the attempt aside with a growl, the force of the blow sending Edith spiraling backward. Yet Edith's resolve did not falter. She righted herself mid-air, her wings spreading wide, and hurtled back toward Bethany. Her hand found purchase this time, seizing her sister's throat in a firm grasp.

The two collided like titans, their forms a blur of motion as they grappled in the night sky. Edith's punches rained down with relentless precision, her divine strength a match for Bethany's infernal fury. But Bethany retaliated with equal ferocity, delivering a vicious double kick that sent Edith careening toward the earth. The impact was cataclysmic, the ground shuddering as she crashed into the scorched earth below, a cloud of dust and ash rising in her wake.

Bethany descended in the aftermath, her wings folding neatly against her back as she landed with practiced ease. She approached Edith with deliberate steps, her eyes glowing with a sinister light. Edith lay crumpled amidst the smoldering ruins, her body trembling as she struggled to rise.

"You shall descend into the inferno," Edith rasped, her voice strained but resolute. Her once luminous wings were now marred with soot and blood, yet the determination in her gaze remained unbroken. "I have shielded thee long enough."

Bethany loomed over her, the glow of the distant flames painting her face in stark, hellish relief. A cruel smile tugged at her lips as she knelt beside her fallen sister. "Shielded me? Oh, sweet Edith, thou hast done naught but hinder my ascent."

* * *

Afore

The air in the modest cabin thickens, choked with the scent of sweat, damp wood, and the metallic tang of blood. Kore moves swiftly, cradling Ara's limp body as she lays her sister onto the fraying cot in the corner of the dimly lit room. The mattress groans beneath Ara's weight, a feeble, sorrowful sound that matches the shudder of her labored breaths.

A fresh pool of golden ichor seeps from the gash in her side, shimmering faintly before it darkens, turns viscous—red. The unnatural shift ripples beneath her skin, her celestial body struggling, failing, to align itself with the cruel, suffocating laws of this foreign realm.

"What devilry works upon me?" Ara's whisper is hoarse, her lips barely parting as the fever rages within her. Sweat clings to her brow, beads of liquid trembling before sliding down the contours of her face. Her once radiant golden eyes, eyes like a dawn unbroken, have begun to cloud—veins creeping pink into the whites, a corruption spreading. Beneath her translucent flesh, dark tendrils pulse, twisting like blackened roots, feeding upon her essence.

Kore's jaw tightens. She dips a cloth into a

basin of chilled water, wrings it hard, and presses it against Ara's searing skin. It is useless. The fever only grows. The veins continue to blacken. Something within her is unraveling.

"The realm infects thee," Kore murmurs, frustration thick in her voice. "Thy body cannot endure this place. If we tarry, thou shalt not adjust—thou shalt perish."

Ara grimaces, her body convulsing as another wave of pain wracks her frame. A ragged breath rattles from her throat before she suddenly seizes Kore's wrist, grip trembling but unyielding.

"There is no escape, sister." Her voice is thin, a whisper threading between gasps. "The machine is broken. No passage remains."

Kore meets her gaze, her own blackened eyes gleaming, burning with something dangerous— something desperate. "Then I shall find a cure."

Ara's lips twitch, curling into a faint, tragic smile—not of amusement, but of inevitability. She is resigned.

"There is none." She closes her eyes for a moment before speaking again, voice faint but unrelenting. "Naught in this accursed world holds the answers we seek. We are not of this place. Nor its understanding."

Kore's fingers curl into fists, her sharp features thrown into jagged relief by the flickering light of the hearth. Her shadow stretches, monstrous against the cabin walls.

"Then it need not come from this realm." The words spill out like a blade unsheathed, cold and certain. "The cure need not belong here. It must only be found."

Her voice hardens, fueled by conviction. "We are not the first of our kind to set foot upon this wretched soil, sister. Thou knowest this as well as I."

A visible shudder passes through Ara. Her golden eyes flicker open again, the firelight dancing within them. A name lingers on her lips—one neither of them dares to speak freely.

"...Father." Her voice is fragile, filled with something tangled between longing and revulsion.

Kore's expression darkens, glacial. Her next words cut sharper than steel.

"Thy father." A bitter smirk ghosts across her lips. "He who claimed dominion over the heavens. He who betrayed his own blood." She leans forward, voice dropping to a venomous whisper. "Yet even he spoke of many realms, many worlds. He swore upon the Vast Sea that an outpost of our people still lingers in this realm. If his words held truth, then I shall find it."

Ara's body trembles, her breath unsteady. "Dost thou believe such a path is easy?" she murmurs, doubt laced with sorrow.

A third voice slithers through the gloom. It does not belong to them.

"If such an outpost exists, the path to it shall be treacherous."

Kore turns sharply.

Ingus steps from the shadows, his presence jarring against the cabin's dim solitude. The dim fire casts ghostly shadows across his face—lined, weary, yet alight with knowing. His thin fingers rest lightly against the doorway, his coat hanging loose upon his frail frame.

"And yet," he continues, his voice slow, measured, "even if thou findest this fabled place, what assurance is there that it shall yield thee what thou seekest?"

Kore's eyes narrow, suspicion cutting through her like ice.

Ingus—one of the town's few doctors, an anomaly himself. A human who both knew of their origins and believed them. That alone made him either a man of wisdom—or a fool courting death.

She does not trust him.

But Ara does. And that is the only reason he still draws breath.

Kore scoffs. "Doubt is the language of men." Her lips curl, fangs glinting in the dim glow. "Accomplishments insurmountable to thy kind are but mere trifles to mine."

Ingus studies her, unflinching beneath her scrutiny. He chooses his words carefully.

"If such a haven doth exist, concealment shall be thy greatest ally."

Kore tilts her head, intrigued despite herself. "Speak plainly."

Ingus takes a step forward. "Names."

A chill rolls through the room.

Kore's expression hardens.

"Thy true names," Ingus says, "are too other-worldly. Too alien. The moment thou utterest them, thou dooms thyselves. Even silence shall not save thee, for thou already doth appear unearthly."

A rasping breath escapes Ara. "What fault lies in our names?" she croaks, the remnants of defiance clinging to her words.

Ingus exhales, rubbing his temples. "They are strange to mortal ears." His voice dips lower. "And in Salem, that which is strange is swiftly branded as witchcraft. Thy survival rests upon thy ability to vanish into the fold."

Kore's black eyes glisten with contempt. "I know naught of earthly names." She spits the words as if they offend her tongue.

Ingus does not hesitate. He reaches into his coat, pulls forth several parchment slips—old, yellowed pages bearing the names of the dead.

His gaze lingers upon one.

"Edith," he says slowly, looking toward Ara. "And Bethany Guzman." His voice is solemn, deliberate. "They were sisters once."

A silence lingers.

Kore tilts her head, testing the name upon her tongue. "Bethany."

A slow, creeping smirk forms on her lips. The name feels foreign—unnatural. But not unworthy.

She turns back to Ingus, stepping closer.

He stiffens.

"I have given thee shelter," he murmurs, "shared my food. I ask only for thy trust." His hands tremble slightly. "What more dost thou require of me?"

Kore's gaze sharpens, hungry as a blade in moonlight. She leans in.

"I require thy word." Her voice drops, low and venomous. "That thou shalt protect her with thy life."

Her eyes darken, flickering with an unnatural glow.

"And if thou dost betray us," she continues, "I shall water the roots of this forest with the crimson slop that spillest from thy treacherous veins."

Ingus pales. His breath shudders—but he does not falter.

He swallows hard and nods. "Thou hast my word."

A long, heavy silence settles.

Kore lingers for only a moment before turning toward the door.

Ara's weak voice halts her.

"Bethany."

Kore pauses, her fingers brushing the splintered frame.

For the briefest second, her expression softens—a whisper of something long buried.

"Rest, sister." Her voice is quiet, almost tender. "Thy trust is not misplaced."

And then—she is gone.

A shadow swallowed by the night.

The wind howls, rattling the cabin walls.

And inside, Ara breathes—a breath caught between life and the abyss.

2

Wings

The forest presses in around her—dark, suffocating, as if the trees themselves conspire to trap the moonlight. Kore—Bethany, she reminds herself, though the name still feels like a borrowed mask—moves through the oppressive blackness with determined strides. Her breath comes in shallow gasps, her legs burning from the strain of relentless, leaping bounds that have carried her miles. Each leap propels her over ravines and fallen trees, but her strength wanes. Every muscle in her body screams for reprieve. She curses the limits of her form as she lands heavily, the damp earth groaning beneath her boots like a living thing.

Time slips away like water through her fingers. The thought of Edith—Ara—dying alone in that wretched cabin claws at her mind. Her sister's transformation has begun. Her once-golden blood darkens to red, her radiant strength withers into a mortal fragility. And yet, Bethany remains untouched by the sickness that ravages their blood-line. The question gnaws at her without mercy: *Why her, and not me?*

The crunch of brittle leaves beneath her boots slices through the forest's eerie silence. For a moment, the world feels unnaturally still. Then it comes—a faint rustling in the underbrush. Deliberate. Heavy. Bethany freezes, her senses sharpening like drawn blades. She is not alone.

Slowly, she turns her head, her dark eyes scanning the shifting shadows. The rustling stops. The forest holds its breath. Bethany exhales sharply and presses forward, her steps careful, deliberate, each one placed with predatory precision. But the sound returns—closer this time. The unmistakable tread of boots grinding against leaves sends a ripple of tension down her spine.

From the darkness, a mounted figure emerges into the clearing. His coat, stitched from worn leather, catches the fragmented moonlight and gleams faintly. He dismounts with practiced ease, the steel of his unsheathed sword catching a glint of silver in the gloom. "Declare thy purpose here, wench," the cavalryman barks, his tone clipped, cold, unwelcoming.

Bethany meets his gaze, her face unflinching,

unreadable. "I owe thee no answers," she replies, her voice as steady as stone. "The woods are no man's, and I walk them as I please."

The cavalryman's lips curl into a sneer. From behind him, more soldiers step from the shadows. Each one dismounts with ghost-like silence, their movements measured, their eyes gleaming like wolves. One holds a flintlock pistol, its barrel polished and gleaming with menace in the pale light.

"Bold words," the leader sneers, "for a lone woman wandering at the devil's hour. Speak plainly, or face the gallows by dawn."

Bethany steps forward, her chin rising with defiance. "Is that thy answer to all thou dost not understand? To string it up and bleed it dry?"

The leader's expression darkens, his knuckles whitening around the hilt of his blade. "Take her," he growls, his voice low and brimming with intent.

The men surge forward, pistols raised. Bethany's muscles coil like springs. She crouches low, instinct screaming to strike, but she restrains herself. She has no time for bloodshed—not tonight. "Stay thy hand!" she shouts, her voice echoing across the clearing. "I seek no quarrel!"

But her words go unanswered.

A deafening shot cracks through the air, the explosion of gunpowder casting a brief, hellish light across the clearing. The bullet strikes her shoulder. She reels back, pain lancing through her, her illusion faltering. Her mortal guise flickers like a candle caught in a wind. Another shot follows, grazing her temple. Bethany stumbles, breath ragged, and her crimson skin begins to surface. Veins, dark as oil, spread beneath her flesh like growing roots.

The men falter, their courage faltering as the truth of her form bleeds into reality. A nightmare stands before them—scarlet flesh, eyes of wrath and ruin. "Demon!" one screams, his voice cracking under the weight of fear.

Bethany straightens, her gaze locking on the leader with a searing glare. "Thou dost name me demon," she growls, voice guttural, distorted. "Yet it is thy hate that breeds monstrosities."

"Kill it!" the commander roars.

The soldiers charge.

Bethany leaps. The force of her jump scatters leaves and debris like a storm's breath. She lands in their midst with a feral snarl, her clawed hands ripping through the first man's chest as if he were made of parchment. Blood erupts in a spray of red mist. The others hesitate, terror coursing through them, but one raises his sword and lunges.

Bethany spins with lethal grace, catching the blade in her bare hand. Her claws tighten around the steel, twisting it free with a piercing screech. In one motion, she drives it into the man's abdomen. Blood spills like wine across her chest, warm and slick, and a growl tears from her throat—deep, primal.

The night becomes a battleground. The air thickens with smoke and blood. Gunshots shatter the silence. Steel clashes against claws. Screams fill the forest, sharp and short-lived. Bethany moves like a tempest, a living weapon of vengeance, carving a path through the men. She ducks under a blade, springs upward, and slashes a throat wide open.

Each kill feeds her. Her strength swells. But so does her rage. Their fear intoxicates her. Their hatred fuels a fire inside her hotter than any wound she's sustained.

Then, it happens.

A sudden, searing agony splits her back. Bethany staggers, her breath catching in her throat. Her body arches. Her claws dig into the earth. Her head throws back and a scream erupts from deep within—raw, primal, deafening. The soldiers pause, frozen mid-motion, the scream rooting them in dread.

A sickening *rip* echoes through the clearing. Something tears free from Bethany's back. She falls to her knees, clawing the soil, as jagged, skeletal wings unfurl behind her. Black, glistening with ichor, they stretch impossibly wide—darker than shadow, heavier than night.

The men stare, paralyzed by the horror.

One soldier turns, fleeing into the woods.

Bethany is faster.

Her wings lash out with crushing force, swiping him down mid-stride. Bones snap. He screams once—and then never again.

The rest scatter, panic erasing any sense of order. But Bethany pursues them with merciless precision, wings slicing through flesh and bone like scythes. "Thou didst seek a demon," she snarls, her voice booming with unearthly power. "Now thou hast found one."

She becomes a whirlwind of wrath. Wings cleave through bodies. Blood rains. Screams are silenced. One by one, they fall—broken, shattered, forgotten.

And then, silence.

Bethany stands alone in the aftermath. Her breath heaves. Her wings drip crimson. The clearing, once sacred and still, is painted in gore. Even the forest seems to recoil, the air thick with dread and disbelief.

She lifts a trembling hand, brushing her fingers along the jagged contours of her wings. A dark smile curves her lips.

He was wrong, she thinks. *Father was wrong. I could grow wings.*

But as she looks down at the carnage she's wrought, the weight of truth sinks deep into her soul. This is no victory.

This is war.

And she is its weapon.

Without a backward glance, she crouches low, her bloodstained wings unfurling once more. Then, with a mighty thrust, she launches into the sky—rising, vanishing into the darkness above, leaving only silence and ruin in her wake.

* * *

The soldier's boots strike the muddy ground with a rhythmic thud, each step jarring his frame as he barrels across the encampment. His breath comes in shallow, uneven gasps, the cold night air burning in his lungs. The scents around him cling to his skin—sweat, damp earth, and the metallic tang of blood. Smoke from dying fires coils upward like lazy phantoms, veiling the stars in thin, shifting curtains. The urgency of the command blazes in his chest, hotter than fear. He cannot falter. Not now. Not with the weight of his orders pressing like iron across his shoulders.

The command tent looms ahead, its dark canvas

walls flickering with torchlight that dances like restless spirits inside. As the soldier nears, something glints in the corner of his eye—a dark, wet smear along the path. He slows instinctively, his boots skidding in the mud before he drops to one knee. Moonlight, faint and sickly, reveals the truth.

Blood.

Fresh, thick, and smeared across the earth like a cruel signature.

A chill spikes down his spine. He swallows hard, the knot in his throat thick with dread, and forces himself to rise. He steps toward the tent entrance with caution, each pace feeling heavier than the last. Whatever lies within, he knows he is bound to face it.

His hand trembles as it parts the flap.

The sight inside steals the breath from his lungs.

Torchlight bathes the scene in a flickering orange glow, casting shadows that stretch like reaching fingers across the canvas walls. Near the center of the tent, a cot sits drenched in blood. Upon it lies a man he recognizes—barely. His tunic is soaked through, the fabric clinging to his chest in gruesome, dark stains. His left arm is missing entirely, torn away in a brutal mess of sinew and exposed bone. Sweat sheens his face, and his eyes roll wildly, unfocused, as he gurgles through lips flecked with blood.

"What devilry is this?" the soldier whispers, the words barely escaping him.

He steps further in, boots making wet, sticky sounds against the blood-slicked ground.

A second soldier looks up from beside the cot, his face carved from grim stone. "Talbot," he says tersely, gesturing toward the dying man. "Report thy men to the commanding officer. Quickly. There's a beast in the wilds. A witch, so they say."

Talbot's jaw tenses. He moves closer, the stench of blood wrapping around him like a smothering cloak. "A witch?" he echoes, disbelief twisting in his voice.

"No." The word cuts through the space like a blade, rough and wet.

The wounded man shifts on the cot, his one remaining hand gripping its edge with trembling fingers. His bloodshot eyes find Talbot's. "It was worse," he rasps, every syllable soaked in pain. "Not a witch… a demon."

The word settles over the tent like a burial shroud.

Nurses freeze mid-motion, their hands suspended over bandages and bowls. The flickering firelight seems to dim. The air grows thick—so thick it might be choking them all.

The soldier tending the cot exchanges a glance with Talbot—one of silent, mutual understanding.

This is no mere tale.

Talbot's heart pounds louder now, a drumbeat of anxiety and purpose. Demons are supposed to be legends, fireside stories meant to frighten children. But there, on that cot, lies a soldier mangled beyond recognition, speaking of horrors no tale could prepare them for.

"A demon," Talbot repeats, voice low and measured. "Thou art certain?"

The dying man nods, just barely. His chest heaves, and his voice strains against the blood filling his throat. "It moved like shadow and fury," he croaks. "Its strength… unholy. It tore through us as though we were naught but parchment. My arm—" He falters, wheezing violently. A nurse leans forward and gently dabs the blood from his lips, but even her practiced hands shake.

Talbot turns to the second soldier, his face pale but composed. "What is thy command?"

The man straightens, his fingers resting uneasily upon the hilt of his blade. "The commanding officer would have us scour the land—every village, every chapel, every home—until this fiend is found. It cannot be allowed to roam."

Talbot's throat tightens at the sheer magnitude of the task. The land is vast. The forest is deep, tangled, and ancient. Every stretch of it could be hiding a horror far beyond their comprehension.

To march into that darkness, to seek this thing beneath the cloak of night, feels like stepping into a grave willingly.

"Dost thou truly believe we stand a chance against such a creature?" he asks, voice edged with doubt.

The other soldier hesitates. His eyes drift toward the cot. Then, slowly, he nods. "If we are to meet our end," he says, "then let it be as soldiers. Not as cowards. But I warn thee, Talbot—this hunt may well be our last."

Talbot's grip tightens around the strap of his musket, his knuckles blanching white. Visions flash through his mind—claws rending flesh, eyes blacker than night, wings ripping through the sky. But beneath the swell of terror, a new flame stirs. *Resolve.* If this demon is what slew his comrades… then it must be stopped. Even if it costs them everything.

He turns toward the tent flap, his jaw clenched. "Then let us ready the men," he says. "If the devil waits in the shadows, then we shall drag it into the light."

The soldier nods once.

With that, Talbot pushes through the flap and steps back into the night.

The cold air hits him like a slap. The wind howls through the encampment, brushing past his cloak and curling around his boots. In the distance, thunder murmurs like a warning. The scent of rain hangs heavy in the breeze, mingling with smoke and ash. Around him, the camp is hushed, the fires reduced to embers, their glow faint and tired—like the hearts of the men who remain.

Talbot pauses at the threshold, his eyes scanning the horizon. Beyond the trees lies the unknown. And somewhere within it, the demon waits.

He breathes deep, steeling himself for what's to come.

War no longer waits on distant shores. Tonight, it walks among them.

* * *

Bethany rips a long strip from the hem of her weathered gray dress, the fabric fraying and tearing like dry parchment in her claws. Her ink-black blood soaks through her blouse, dark and viscous, staining the coarse linen like spilled oil across brittle parchment. The smell is sharp—bitter, metallic, and unmistakably wrong. She cinches the makeshift bandage around her shoulder, tugging it tight with impatient precision. Pain flares in her torn flesh, but she ignores it. Her thoughts churn, not with fear, but with the lingering thrill of what has just awakened.

Her wings.

Above her, the night sky yawns vast and ominous, a canvas of ink behind the silver gleam of a swollen moon. The stars flicker faintly behind a veil of mist. Trees surround her like a ring of skeletal watchers, their gnarled limbs clawing toward the heavens. Bethany crouches low, her knees bending, her powerful legs coiling like springs prepared to snap. Her wings fold tightly behind her, their dark, leathery surface twitching with anticipation, still pulsing with the memory of their violent birth.

With a thunderous leap, she launches skyward.

The forest floor shudders beneath the force of her ascent, leaves spiraling into the air like startled birds. Her wings rip outward mid-flight, catching the wind in a violent snap as she slices through the night. She rises higher and higher, faster with each beat. The world below fades into a blur of shadows and silence. For a heartbeat—no, two—she is weightless, boundless, free. A living silhouette crossing the face of the moon.

Then it hits her.

From the black void of the sky, a blinding lance of searing light crashes down. It moves faster than thought, striking her right wing like judgment from the heavens. The bolt burns through her flesh, ripping her flight from her in an instant. Agony detonates in her body. She lets out a scream that splits the night—a guttural cry of fury and pain.

Her wing buckles. Her body twists mid-air, and she plummets.

She crashes to earth like a fallen star. The impact sends tremors through the forest floor, cratering the soil beneath her. Smoke curls from the scorched wound in her wing, rising like a funeral prayer. For a moment, she lies still—chest heaving, body quaking, blood bubbling at the corner of her mouth. Every breath tastes like metal.

She pushes herself up with trembling arms, her claws digging into the dirt. Her head spins. Her shoulder screams with pain. But her mind races faster still. The weapon that struck her—*that* was no musket. No gunpowder. No lead. Mortal men wield nothing so precise, so devastating. She *feels* the residue, still humming in the air, as if the weapon left behind a ghost of itself.

This was no accident.

Bethany inhales sharply, letting the forest's scent flood her senses—damp moss, decaying bark, old blood—and something else. Something foreign. Something *wrong*. A chemical tang. Cold. Familiar. Her lip curls back into a snarl.

A hunter.

Before she can rise to her full height, the wind shifts. The scent grows stronger—sharper—right before the silence shatters.

The creature explodes from the underbrush.

A black, hulking shadow crashes through the thicket with terrifying speed. Its sinewy body seems to ripple like smoke, its jagged claws glinting in the moonlight. Its face is eyeless, save for two hollow voids that burn with a pale, hellish fire. It is hunger given form.

Bethany reacts on instinct.

She twists, barely dodging the swipe of its claws. Her injured wings twitch as they attempt to lift her, but the pain keeps her grounded. She leaps backward, snarling. The beast lunges again, faster this time. Claws slash the air just inches from her throat. She snaps her wings open and forces herself upward—desperate for air, for distance—but the monster is unrelenting.

It springs.

The two collide mid-air, and the world tilts.

They crash back to the earth, the impact reverberating through the forest like thunder. Bethany slams into the dirt with bruising force, her ribs screaming as the air is driven from her lungs. She scrambles, clawing at the earth, her body aching as she rises. The shadow beast looms over her, hot breath washing over her skin in waves. Its growl is low and guttural, vibrating through the bones of the trees.

Bethany turns and bolts.

She hurls herself into a sprint, her feet pounding over roots and fallen branches. The forest blurs past her. The underbrush lashes at her ankles, tearing her dress. Behind her, the hunter follows—its snarls echoing like a storm rolling over the hills. Every step feels heavier. Her wings flare again, the injured one trailing, dragging like a dead limb. She jumps and stumbles into flight for half a second.

Just long enough to clear a gnarled tree before gravity reclaims her.

Then the bolt hits.

A second beam of radiant energy strikes her from behind. Her scream rips through the forest. She careens forward uncontrollably, tumbling through air and shadow until—

Crash.

Her body slams into something broad and muscular and warm.

A horse.

The beast rears in panic, shrieking. Bethany crumples at its feet, limp and bloodied, while the rider—a soldier—topples from the saddle. His body slams into the dirt, armor rattling against the ground in a deafening clatter.

Bethany lies motionless.

Her limbs tremble. Her vision dims. The last sound she hears before slipping into darkness is the echo of the horse's frantic cries.

The soldier groans beside her. The horse stomps and bucks wildly, drawing the attention of others from the camp. Torches approach. Shadows grow longer.

The soldiers arrive—and stop dead in their tracks.

There she lies.

Crimson-skinned. Barely breathing. Blood pooled beneath her, glistening like oil in the torch-light. Her body is broken. Her form is monstrous.

Talbot is among them.

He clutches his musket with trembling hands. His eyes widen at the sight before him—of the red-skinned creature sprawled at the horse's feet. "What... what devilry is this?" he breathes, voice cracking under the weight of the moment.

Then the forest falls silent.

Utterly still. The kind of silence that carries weight.

Talbot swallows hard. He raises his weapon, aiming toward the tree line. His voice wavers. "Show thyself... or be fired upon!"

The answer comes swift and terrible.

A figure steps from the shadows.

Towering. Inhuman.

The Kelxsiar warrior strides into the clearing, its form grotesque and gleaming with an otherworldly sheen. Its armor shifts like fluid metal, glinting beneath the torchlight in hues no mortal metal has ever known. The soldiers freeze, their weapons held fast in shaking hands.

Its eyes glow like coals—burning low, slow, steady. Its maw stretches in a jagged, toothy grin. It releases a low, rattling growl that hums through the ground like a fault line trembling.

Talbot's hands sweat against the musket. His finger flinches toward the trigger.

"Hold," he whispers to himself, a plea and a command in one.

The Kelxsiar tilts its head.

Its gaze settles not on Talbot—but on Bethany.

And for a moment, the world forgets to breathe.

Then the Kelxsiar opens its maw.

And roars.

A sound that rips through the trees and the sky and the souls of every man present. A cry like a thousand damned souls wailing in unison.

The forest pulses with tension, alive with silence that feels like a scream withheld. The trees loom higher, and the moon seems to shrink beneath the pressure of what now stands among them. Every leaf, every gust of wind carries the weight of something unnatural.

Talbot steps forward, his pistol raised, the barrel trembling ever so slightly in his hands despite the steel in his gaze. His breath fogs in the cold night air, each exhale a ghost of fear trying to escape him. "Stand down!" he barks. The command rings clear—but beneath it, his voice wavers, straining beneath the gravity of what looms ahead.

The Kelxsiar warrior does not flinch.

It towers before him, grotesque and magnificent, its form seemingly forged from sinew, smoke, and nightmare. The moonlight refuses to touch it—absorbed into the shadow-woven armor clinging to its angular limbs. Jagged plates of crude metal mesh with glistening tissue, pulsing with veins of black ichor. Its hollow eyes burn dimly—like the dying coals of a forgotten fire. A twisted snarl peels back its lips, revealing a mouth full of jagged, glinting teeth.

A deep growl rumbles from the beast's core, low and long, vibrating through the ground beneath them. Its head tilts unnaturally. The sinews in its neck twitch. Its voice grates from its throat, fractured and inhuman, like stone being broken by hand. "Your weapons… weak," it growls, its grasp of the language rough and uneven. "They not shield… the stench… of your fear."

The soldiers surrounding Talbot shift, their muskets creaking and cuirasses clinking in nervous rhythm. Their formation fractures slightly, the façade of control slipping. Talbot clenches his jaw and tightens his grip on the pistol. His finger hovers near the trigger. "You smell fear?" he replies, voice tight. "What devil art thou?"

The Kelxsiar lifts its chin. Its snarl curls wider, twisted with malice. It straightens its massive body with slow, deliberate menace. "We are... from darkest realms," it says, each word grinding like rusted gears. "No quarrel... with your kind. We hunt... one from our realm."

Talbot follows its gaze as it shifts to the figure lying motionless in the dirt.

Bethany.

Her body is bloodied, her crimson skin a grotesque contrast against the pale earth. Her wings lie limp, mangled shadows splayed wide across the ground. She doesn't move.

"Her?" he asks, though the word comes more as a breath than a question—laced with accusation, disbelief, and caution.

The Kelxsiar's burning gaze lingers on Bethany. It takes one step forward—slow, deliberate. The soldiers flinch as one, weapons raised, every eye fixed on the towering threat. The Kelxsiar growls, a low, displeased sound like a warning bell before the storm.

"No," it spits, the word thick with disdain. "She is... of no use. She must be... executed."

A chill settles over the clearing.

Talbot's eyes narrow. Confusion surges—but so does a flicker of defiance. "She is our prisoner," he says, louder now, the steel returning to his voice. "She hath slain our men. She must hang by our law."

The Kelxsiar pauses. Its head jerks slightly, its alien form twitching as though weighing his words, or perhaps translating them. Its eyes flick between Talbot and Bethany's broken body. Then, after a beat that stretches too long, it speaks again.

"Take her," it rumbles at last. "She is weak. She is not... the one we seek."

The words sink in slowly, heavy as stone dropped in water.

Talbot exchanges a glance with the other soldiers. Unease gnaws at his insides, spreading like frost. "There are... others?" he asks, cautious now. A tremor of something darker stirs beneath his curiosity.

"Yes," the Kelxsiar hisses, leaning forward slightly, its ember eyes glowing brighter. "This one... not same. She corrupted. Half-born. But... another. Pure blood. We have... latched to her scent."

Pure blood.

The words slam into Talbot like a musket ball to the chest. He stares at Bethany—still motionless, her body twitching faintly with shallow breaths. Crimson skin. Dark wings. And yet... she is not the one.

Something worse is out there.

Something stronger.

The Kelxsiar steps back, its form blending again with the shadows that cling to it like a shroud. Its gaze never breaks from Talbot's. "You meddle... in what not for you," it warns, voice like gravel and death. "Leave this forest... or burn with it."

And with that, it turns.

It moves with impossible grace, vanishing into the treeline as if swallowed by the night itself. One moment it stands—monolithic and terrible. The next, it is gone. Not even a footprint remains.

The clearing falls into stunned stillness.

No one breathes.

No one speaks.

Even the wind seems to hush.

Talbot lowers his pistol slowly, hand slack with exhaustion. Around him, the soldiers remain frozen, muskets still aimed at the place where the Kelxsiar disappeared. The air feels thinner, like the creature took part of the night with it.

The forest seems to exhale.

The oppressive pressure lifts, but only slightly—replaced by an unease that coils through the camp like smoke from a smoldering fire. Talbot turns at last, voice low and firm. "Secure the prisoner," he says, nodding toward Bethany's body. "And ready thy arms. If there be more of her kind… we may yet meet them."

The men move hesitantly, approaching Bethany's form with the same caution one might use near a venomous snake. Their faces are pale. Their steps reluctant. Fear has not left them—it simply wears a new name now.

Talbot remains where he is, eyes fixed on the trees.

He stares at the place where the Kelxsiar disappeared. The words echo again in his mind, twisted and damning.

Pure blood.

His grip tightens on the stock of his weapon.

If *this* creature was not the threat… if *she* was not the one they feared…

Then something worse waits in the dark.

And it knows they're here.

* * *

The cabin feels stifling, the air thick with the mingled scents of sweat, sickness, and damp, rotting wood. Shadows cling to the corners like cobwebs, and every breath tastes of fever. Edith—once Ara—lies trembling atop the hard cot, her body a fading echo of the celestial force she once was. Her golden blood has long since turned crimson, and her once-vibrant aura has dimmed to the faint glow of a dying ember. The bedding beneath her clings to her skin, soaked with perspiration that glistens like oil under the sway of the lantern above. It rocks gently on its iron hook, casting flickers of sickly yellow light across the cabin walls. Her breath rattles in her chest—thin, shallow, like the wind whispering through broken shutters.

Ingus paces the room in agitated circles, his hands tearing through his hair, his brow damp and creased with dread. The words Bethany left him with echo in his mind, repeating over and over like a curse: *If she dies, you die.* He can feel those words branding themselves into his bones, turning every heartbeat into a warning. Each glance toward Edith's frail, trembling form strips another layer of resolve from his soul.

"Water..." she croaks, her voice so weak it's barely more than a scrape of wind across dry leaves. Her lips are cracked and pale, her mouth moving slowly as she struggles to speak.

Ingus lunges into motion, nearly tripping over himself as he grabs the canteen from the rough-hewn table. He rushes to her side, tipping the water to her mouth with trembling hands. As she drinks, his gaze flicks toward the cabin's only window—a narrow pane warped by time. "Where dost thou think thy sister is?" he whispers, voice stretched thin with nerves and the weight of a question he's too afraid to answer.

Edith swallows slowly. Her eyelids flutter open, unfocused at first, then sharpening just enough to hold meaning. "Wherever she needs to be," she whispers, her tone faint but threaded with resolve, even as her fragile body betrays her.

But the moment hangs only for a breath before it's shattered.

A rustling outside splits the stillness—too heavy, too deliberate to be wind or beast. Ingus stiffens. He steps cautiously toward the window, peering through the warped glass. His breath fogs the pane as he stares into the trees. Shadows move just beyond the treeline. Human shadows.

"There's someone here," he hisses, his voice a strained whisper barely louder than the breath it rides on.

Edith stirs weakly, her head turning toward him. "Tend to me," she commands, her voice still frail but firm with purpose. "Act as though all is well. If luck favors us, they may pass by."

Ingus hesitates—then shakes his head, eyes wide. Panic begins to rise within him like water breaching a dam. "It is the village police," he breathes. "They circle the cabin… Something is amiss."

He barely finishes the thought when a thunderous knock booms against the door, rattling the hinges and driving a spike of fear into the room. Ingus staggers back, pale as ash, clutching the back of a chair as though it might anchor him.

"Oh God…"

"To me, Ingus!" Edith commands, her voice cutting through the room like a blade. Weak though she may be, the force in her words is undeniable. Ingus obeys at once, retreating to her side like a man seeking sanctuary. He crouches low beside her cot, eyes darting between her and the door.

Edith draws a breath and calls out, steady and cold, "Enter, if thou must."

The door creaks open.

Two figures step inside, and with them, the air grows heavier. They are tall and broad-shouldered, their forms wrapped in thick leather coats re-inforced with iron-studded belts. Their wide-brimmed hats shadow their eyes, but the glint beneath reveals suspicion—and something colder. Contempt. Their hands hover near their holstered pistols, fingers twitching with practiced readiness. Behind them, a crowd of villagers lingers, their faces pale and pinched, their eyes wide with mor-bid anticipation.

One of the officers—taller, with a gaunt face and a scar bisecting his chin—shuts the door behind him. His gaze lands on Ingus with instant disdain.

"Thou may leave, doctor," he says, his tone like frost over stone. "She is no longer thy concern."

Ingus straightens, though his voice shakes. "She is gravely ill. It is imperative I remain by her side."

The second officer—Murphy—sneers. "Spare us thy theater. She is a liar and a wench, and thou art a fool for defending her."

Edith shifts on the cot, pushing herself upright with visible strain. Her body trembles, but her voice holds firm. "What accusation dost thou bring to my door?" she asks, her tone calm yet biting, like iron beneath velvet.

Murphy steps forward, his boots thudding across the floorboards. "Witchcraft," he declares, letting the word hang like a noose. It fills the room, suffocating and final.

Edith's lips twitch into a faint smile—cold, sardonic. "Art thou certain of this claim?" she asks, a slight tilt to her head. Despite the sweat on her brow, she wears defiance like armor.

"Do not feign innocence, jezebel!" Murphy snaps. His voice cracks with rising fury. "Witnesses saw thee and thy sister take flight—wings as white as moonlight. Deny it if thou dare."

"Impossible," Ingus blurts, his voice loud, raw with disbelief. His fear trembles beneath his words, but they carry weight nonetheless.

"Impossible indeed," Murphy retorts, sneering.

"For those who walk with saints. But thou—thou art not of us. Thy defense damns thee further."

The other officer, Cooper, who has remained still until now, speaks with a calm, deliberate voice. "The punishment for witchcraft is clear. Hanging. By the neck. Until death."

Ingus's throat tightens. "There are no witches here," he murmurs, though the strength in his voice has faded.

Murphy steps closer, pointing a gloved finger at Edith like a judge passing sentence. "I trust the word of godly men over that of heathens. Arrest her. She shall face judgment."

At his word, the crowd outside surges into the cabin. Their hands are calloused, their grips merciless. They seize Edith from the cot, her body folding with pain. She cries out, but still she struggles. Her legs buckle beneath her, dragging limply across the wooden floor.

"No!" Ingus shouts, lunging. He pushes one of them hard. "Stop this madness!"

Murphy wheels around and slams him back with a brutal shove. Ingus hits the wall, air leaving his lungs in a ragged grunt.

"Defend her again," Murphy growls, voice low and deadly, "and thou shalt share her fate."

Ingus freezes. His fists clench. His breath comes in hard, panicked bursts as he watches them drag

Edith to the door. She doesn't scream. She doesn't cry. Her head lolls—but her eyes find his.

And in them, there is fire.

A promise.

This is not the end.

The door slams shut behind them, and the noise echoes like a coffin nail being driven into wood. Ingus stands motionless. Then, slowly, he sinks to his knees. The cabin feels emptier than death. The distant roar of the mob fades, swallowed by the trees—but their hatred lingers. It clings to the walls. It lives in the shadows.

He stares at the cot.

At the imprint her body has left.

Her scent remains. Her blood.

And her defiance.

It rings in his ears like a bell. And he knows—

The storm has only just begun.

3

Precious Humanity

The pit is a hellish circle of dirt and blood, its edges bordered by jagged rocks and the jeering faces of townsfolk and soldiers alike. Torches flicker in the cool night air, casting grotesque shadows that writhe like specters across the pit walls. Bethany hits the ground hard, her body skidding in the dust. She groans as the rough earth scrapes her skin, but she pushes herself to her knees, her crimson form catching the firelight in a ghastly glow. Her wings hang limp at her back—dark, tattered, twitching weakly with each strained breath.

Above her, the soldiers sneer, their weapons gleaming wickedly in the torchlight. The crowd's chants rise in volume—a cacophony of hate and bloodlust. Bethany knows this theater of cruelty well; she has been its subject before in her realm.

Now, this world echoes that torment with chilling familiarity. She rises slowly, eyes scanning the leering faces, her gaze sharp, unyielding.

The pit opens again.

Soldiers drag forth a dark-skinned woman, her wrists bound in rusted shackles that clank with each step. They shove her forward with brutal force, sending her sprawling into the dirt. Her eyes dart wildly, her breath ragged as she scrambles to her knees. Fear radiates from her like heat—her trembling form a stark contrast to the defiance burning in Bethany's gaze.

"Runaway and an animal! Serves thee right!" one soldier bellows, his voice met with raucous laughter from the crowd. The soldiers move quickly, unlocking the shackles; the iron drops to the ground with a harsh clatter. The woman flinches, rubbing at her raw wrists, but Bethany sees it instantly—this is no beast. There is no feral hatred in her gaze. Only confusion. Only fear.

"Fight, wretched beast!" another soldier shouts, his voice slicing through the crowd's din like a blade. He points his musket at Bethany, the barrel glinting menacingly. The command hangs in the air like venom, and the crowd howls its approval— eager for carnage.

Bethany turns her scornful gaze toward the soldier. Her eyes narrow into slits. "No," she says flatly, her voice cutting through the noise like a wind through splintered glass. Calm—but unmovable.

The soldier sneers. "Thou art a fool if thou thinkest we shan't shoot thee."

Bethany does not flinch. Her gaze drifts to the terrified woman, who trembles so violently it seems her bones might rattle loose. "If thy intent is to shoot me," Bethany says, her tone deliberate, low, "then shoot. But let her go."

The crowd's laughter curdles into a cruel, mocking din. A wiry soldier with a vicious grin leans over the edge of the pit. "Bidwell! Fire upon her at my word!" he barks, musket raised and primed.

Bethany's stare remains steady. Her voice brims with disdain. "She is afraid. It is plain thou hast tortured her. And thou wouldst have me punish her further?" Her head tilts slightly, her tone now razor-sharp. "Thy quarrel is not mine. Do as thou wilt—but not by my hand."

"She is a runaway!" the lead soldier spits. "She must be punished!"

Bethany's lips curl into a humorless smile. "Not by me."

"Fire!" the soldier roars.

The first rifle cracks. The shot echoes like thunder.

The bullet strikes Bethany square in the chest.

Her body jolts, black blood spraying into the dust. She grits her teeth, a guttural growl bubbling up from her throat. She staggers—but does not fall. Her blazing eyes lock onto the soldier with unrelenting fury. Then she steps forward.

Another shot rings out. This one tears into her back.

Bethany cries out—a piercing shriek that silences the crowd. She whirls, teeth bared in a feral snarl, blood dripping onto the ground, pooling like tar. The woman behind her cowers, frozen in awe and terror. A creature stands before her—something beyond mortal, beyond comprehension, who defies pain, who defies death.

The soldiers hesitate, fingers trembling on their weapons. "Still she stands," one mutters, voice cracking with fear.

Bethany's growl deepens. Her steps quicken into a furious charge toward the lead soldier. Her body is a blur of rage and vengeance, her claws carving the air as she closes the gap. The soldier's eyes widen in terror—but before she reaches him, another shot fires.

The bullet hits her square in the face.

Bethany's body collapses in the dirt with a heavy, lifeless thud.

Silence falls. The echo of the final shot lingers, ringing in the ears of every onlooker. Bethany's form lies motionless, her crimson skin streaked with black blood as it seeps into the thirsty earth. In the pit, the woman whimpers, clutching her knees, her eyes fixed on the monstrous stillness.

Cautiously, the lead soldier approaches. His musket remains raised. He prods Bethany's body with the barrel, his breath shallow, every nerve taut with dread. The crowd leans in, spellbound—half afraid, half yearning for one final moment of horror.

Then it begins.

From the shadows of the pit, a low, guttural growl rises.

It is faint—at first.

But it grows.

It reverberates through the night like the distant rumble of a storm. Bethany's body twitches. Her fingers curl into the dirt.

The growl crescendos into a roar—wild, ancient, vengeful.

Soldiers stumble back in terror.

Her blackened eyes snap open. They burn with hatred.

Though her body is broken, her rage endures.

The pit is quiet now, the crowd's jeers muffled by the hush of distance and dread. Bethany lies in the dust, her body battered and still, her crimson skin streaked with thick, blackened blood. The air hangs heavy—clogged with the metallic tang of spilled life and the slow rot of suffering. Her chest rises once more. Slowly. Then again.

Her eyes flicker open.

They shine with that same otherworldly black, deep as void, vast as vengeance. She inhales sharply, her senses honed despite the pain radiating through every muscle, every bone.

Before her, the woman still stands. Barely. Her figure is gaunt, fragile, trembling. Dark skin marred by a lattice of scars that speak of a long, cruel life. Her eyes dart around the pit's edge, wide and haunted, as if expecting the soldiers to return and drag her off at any moment. Yet she remains. Still breathing. Still watching.

Their gazes meet.

"What... what are you?" the woman whispers, voice barely audible—quivering with awe and terror. The words drip with an accent Bethany doesn't recognize. Strange syllables. Familiar pain.

Bethany pushes herself up, slow and deliberate, every movement an act of defiance. "Not what thou art," she replies bitterly, her tone etched in iron.

The woman's eyes flood with tears, but she holds her ground. "Yes... aye," she murmurs, her voice halting, like her own words betray her. "You...

coulda killed me. They… they would've freed you."

Bethany tilts her head, studying her. "No. They would not," she says, voice low, resolute. "They imprison me for what I am. For my skin. And thee? Why dost thou stand here?"

The woman looks down at the dirt beneath her feet. "For the same," she admits quietly. "For my skin. For what I am… where I come from."

Bethany's expression softens, if only slightly. Her tone carries a weariness now—an unspoken kinship. "Where is it? Thy home?"

"Far," the woman says, voice barely above a breath. "Far from here. Across waters, they say. I scarce recall it now."

Bethany nods slowly, her breath catching in her throat. "Same," she says after a pause, voice laced with that same unspoken ache. "What do they call thee?"

"Kamillah," the woman says, her name trembling from her lips as if it holds the weight of lifetimes. She extends her shackled hands, wrists raw and torn. The scars on her arms and shoulders are brutal, unapologetic—each one a story, a scream, a sentence passed by a cruel world.

Bethany's warrior's gaze flicks over them. Kamillah is small. Broken. But she has endured. She bears no weapon. No hatred. Just wounds. And survival. Bethany sees it—this woman is not a soldier. She is not a killer. She is a victim.

"They're coming back," Kamillah says, voice catching as fresh tears spill down her cheeks. "They'll want me to fight you. They'll make you kill me."

Bethany exhales slowly, her fingers curling against the ground. "I shan't fight thee," she says, pushing herself to her feet with a trembling strength. "I'll not give them the pleasure."

Kamillah shakes her head. Her body trembles beneath its own weight. "You can't run. They'll kill you. They'll hunt you. Like they hunted me."

Bethany's lips twist into a grim smile. Her teeth catch the faint torchlight, sharp and white like bones in moonlight. "They'll wish they could," she says, darkly. "There is much thou dost not know of me—of my lineage, of my strength."

Kamillah stares at her, confusion and the faintest flicker of something else blooming behind her tears. "Where… where you come from… do they do this?" she asks, uncertain.

"They do worse," Bethany answers, voice low and haunted. Memories of her realm churn like a storm behind her eyes. "They imprison those like me. Anomalies. They call us abominations." Her gaze falls to Kamillah's arms. "But thou art no threat. Thou hast harmed no one."

Kamillah hesitates—then lowers her eyes.

Slowly, she peels down the torn remnants of her blouse, revealing her back.

The scars there are savage.

Deep. Fresh and infected. The skin raised and livid in angry red ridges. A brutal history carved into flesh.

"They… they torture us," Kamillah says, her voice thick with sorrow. "For nothin'. For just… bein'."

Bethany's jaw tightens. Rage simmers beneath her skin like fire in a furnace. She steps closer, voice softer but sharpened with steel. "Run," she says.

Kamillah flinches, recoiling. "I tried," she whispers, her shame laid bare. "They catch me. Lash me. Kill you if you try."

Bethany kneels down beside her, her voice quiet, resolute. "No," she says. "Not this time. This time, thou shalt run with me."

Kamillah's head shakes violently. "No! They'll catch us both! Lash me again—kill you outright!"

Bethany rises to her full height, her silhouette casting a long shadow across the pit. "Let them try," she says. Her voice is a growl now, thick with fury. "They think they own us. They think their laws are divine." Her fists clench. "But freedom is not granted, Kamillah. It is taken. And if thou must run for it—then no rule of theirs should hold sway over thee."

The words hang in the pit like thunder before a storm. Kamillah stares at Bethany, tears still falling—but something else stirs behind them now.

It is not quite hope. Not yet.

But it might be the beginning of it.

Above them, the soldiers' voices echo—closer now. The edge of the pit glows again with torch-light. Shadows dance.

Bethany plants herself in front of Kamillah, wings twitching at her back, blood still trailing from her wounds. Her stance hardens, jaw set.

"Stay behind me," she says, voice like stone.

"Let them see," she growls, "what true defiance looks like."

The soldiers approach the pit like wolves circling wounded prey, their boots crunching over the dirt with slow, menacing deliberation. Their faces glisten with sweat, and their eyes burn with the cruel anticipation of violence. Voices rise—jeers, shouted commands, barked threats—all echoing through the clearing like the guttural chants of a blood cult. Above, the sky hangs low and choked with clouds, smothering the moon and cloaking the scene in an oppressive, suffocating darkness.

Bethany's chest heaves as she pushes herself fully upright, her crimson skin glistening with a sheen of sweat and congealed black blood. Her eyes, once hollow shadows, begin to glow from within. A fiery red radiance replaces the void, flaring like embers beneath a dying flame. Her lips curl back, and her teeth lengthen into vampiric points, jagged and glistening. The soldiers falter. Their confident strides slow as they take in the grotesque transformation before them.

One soldier stops short, his musket trembling in his hands. His face contorts with dread, his mouth parting in silent horror as he stares directly into Bethany's burning gaze. The moment stretches— thick and heavy—as fear crawls into their bones. Behind Bethany, Kamillah cowers, her frame con- vulsing as her bare feet scramble backward in the dirt. Her wide eyes dart between the soldiers and the nightmare rising in front of her.

Bethany's back arches violently.

A sickening, wet *rip* echoes through the pit as her wings erupt from her flesh—leathery, grotesque things that unfurl like monstrous limbs, glistening with ichor and twitching as though with minds of their own. Kamillah gasps, both hands flying to her mouth as she watches in mute terror. One of the wings lashes forward with terrifying speed, coiling around the nearest soldier like a serpent. He doesn't even have time to scream properly. His voice cracks mid-howl before the wing tightens and *tears him apart*, his body ripping open in a grotesque spray of blood and sinew. The pit is painted red.

The remaining soldiers break from their stupor, shouting in alarm. Their fear erupts into a frenzy of panicked violence.

"OPEN FIRE!" one bellows, voice cracking as he raises his musket.

Gunfire explodes across the pit.

The flashes of flame light Bethany's form in jolts of orange and gold. Bullets tear into her—one through the ribs, another through her thigh, several into her arms and abdomen. Black ichor pours from the wounds, thick as tar.

But she does not slow.

Bethany's fury grows with every strike. Her body pulses with an otherworldly light that begins to flare from within—an aura of raw, celestial wrath. The glow intensifies, brightening until it envelops her like a second skin, a barrier against the mortal world's weapons.

Suddenly, the aura flares outward.

The bullets bounce harmlessly off the shimmering veil, clinking to the ground like spent coins.

The soldiers cry out in terror, realizing their muskets are worthless.

Bethany's wings strike again.

One cleaves through a man's shoulder with surgical violence; another slices through bone and spine as if through paper. The pit becomes a slaughterhouse. Screams rise, choked and wet. Blood pools thick in the dirt. Broken bodies collapse one after another, until silence begins to reclaim the pit—broken only by Kamillah's soft sobbing.

From the rear of the clearing, panicked voices cry for reinforcements. Soldiers trip over each other, desperate to flee the carnage. Their torches sway wildly in the dark.

Bethany turns. Her crimson face is streaked with ichor, her glowing eyes searing into Kamillah's.

She extends a clawed hand.

"Come with me!" she snarls. Her voice is sharp, commanding—yet not unkind.

Kamillah freezes. Her breath catches. Every instinct screams at her to run, yet her body will not obey. She stares at the monster that just saved her life.

"Kamillah," Bethany growls again, softer now, her voice almost pleading. "I will not harm thee. Take my hand."

Tears stream freely down Kamillah's cheeks. She reaches out, shackled hands trembling, and grasps Bethany's claw.

"Can thou…can thou truly fly?" she asks, voice quivering with awe and disbelief.

Bethany nods, a swift, solemn motion. "Aye. But

we must make haste, or they will shoot us from the heavens."

With a jerk, she hauls Kamillah to her feet. Her wings fold protectively around them both as they scramble out of the pit. The crowd above has scattered. Most torches are distant now, bobbing through the trees like frightened spirits.

They bolt for the woods.

The dense thicket offers cover, but the terrain is cruel—roots rising like twisted hands, underbrush clawing at their legs. Bethany moves with speed and ferocity, each stride steady, calculated. Kamillah stumbles behind, her breath ragged, chains dragging through the dirt.

"Kamillah, keep up!" Bethany barks, glancing back with urgency.

"I... I can't!" Kamillah cries out. Her shackles rattle with each desperate step, and her weakened body lurches with exhaustion.

Bethany whips around, fury flashing in her eyes. She extends a clawed hand toward the chains.

The shackles begin to glow—soft at first, then bright. The iron heats and warps. In a moment, the metal melts clean away, dripping into the soil like molten wax.

"Run!" Bethany commands. She grabs Kamillah's arm and pulls her forward with renewed urgency.

Behind them, gunfire erupts.

The blasts crack like thunder, bullets zipping past their heads, striking trees, splintering bark, hissing through the leaves. The night explodes in chaos.

A bullet slams into Kamillah's leg.

She screams—a raw, piercing sound—and collapses just feet from the edge of the tree line.

Bethany skids to a halt, wings flaring as she spins back. "Kamillah!" she cries out, her voice thick with panic. She sees the blood spreading, the agony in Kamillah's face.

Torches are closing in.

Shadows leap across the forest floor.

Kamillah meets her gaze, her face twisted with pain and surrender. "Go," she whispers, her voice barely audible over the chaos. "They'll kill us both."

Bethany's claws dig into the dirt. Her body shakes—not with fear, but with the war raging inside her. Her instincts scream to fight. Her heart screams to stay. But the moment gives her no mercy.

Gunfire cracks again.

A bullet grazes Bethany's wing. She snarls and clenches her jaw.

One final look at Kamillah.

Then—

Bethany leaps.

Her wings blast open with a deafening *whoosh*, and she rockets into the sky, her body cutting through the darkness like a blade. She ascends fast, higher, past the torchlight, past the trees, into the veiled cloud cover above.

Below, Kamillah disappears into the chaos.

Soldiers swarm around her, their torches casting long shadows as they surround her broken form.

The forest goes quiet.

The screams fade.

And Bethany—bleeding, furious, alone—soars through the choking black sky.

The night swallows her whole.

Above the canopy, she flies faster, breath tight, heart pounding. Guilt coils in her chest like a living serpent. Kamillah's face—wounded, terrified—burns behind her eyes.

A face she could not save.

* * *

The gavel comes down with a deafening crack, echoing through the stone-walled chamber like a thunderclap splitting the sky. The priest—an almost goblin-like figure with sagging, wart-covered skin—leans forward from his pulpit, his hunched frame casting a grotesque shadow in the torchlight. His yellowed eyes gleam with unbridled hatred as they fixate on Edith. Each flicker of fire exaggerates the cruel lines carved into his face.

Around him, the townspeople mutter and hiss like a nest of serpents. Their faces twist with fear, suspicion, and malice. The smell of sweat and old wood saturates the air. Edith sits at the chamber's center, shackled tightly to a splintered wooden chair. Her once-luminous golden skin now appears pallid, touched by illness, though it still faintly glistens beneath the flickering flame. Her eyes, dimmed by sickness but steady, rest on her bound wrists. Her expression remains unbroken—unimpressed by the venom surrounding her.

"Thy sister hath been seen!" the priest bellows, spit flying from his cracked lips. His voice, shrill and trembling with grotesque fervor, ricochets against the chamber walls. "Wings of the wicked—born of demons and nurtured by Hell itself! She hath shown her true nature! That of a witch! That of a beast!"

A sharp voice rises from the mob. "She hides her sister's wickedness! She dares not show her own wings for they carry the same cursed mark!" A stout, sharp-faced townswoman jabs a crooked finger at Edith.

The crowd erupts.

Accusations fly like daggers, curses thick as ash in the air. The room becomes a storm of outrage, their shouts feeding off one another until it becomes one deafening roar of righteous cruelty.

Edith lifts her head slowly. Her body trembles under the weight of sickness and chain, but her voice cuts through the chaos with eerie calm.

"My sister and I are many things," she says, her words slow and even, "much of which thy kind cannot begin to comprehend. But we are not the witches thou wouldst label us."

The mob howls in fury.

But the priest is louder. His twisted hand slams against the pulpit with a meaty *crack*, bringing sudden silence.

"Enough of thy lies, whore!" he screeches, veins bulging in his neck. "We have heard enough! Thy judgment is swift and just. By unanimous decree, the witch before us shall hang until her cursed neck snaps like a brittle branch!"

Edith doesn't flinch.

She lets the moment breathe.

Then, with a weak yet defiant sneer, she rasps, "I am already dying."

The priest's cracked lips peel into a deeper, crueler smile. "Then may thy wickedness hasten the process. Guards—throw her in the cell. Let her rot till the gallows are set."

Time becomes meaningless inside the suffocating dark of the cell.

Moisture seeps from the stone walls, and the air is thick with the stench of mold, urine, and old death. Rats scurry unseen. Edith lies curled on a splintered cot, her frame thin and trembling. Waves of pain roll through her in cruel rhythm. The straw beneath her scratches at her skin, offering no comfort—only insult. Iron shackles bite into her wrists, leaving angry, swollen welts. And yet her mind refuses to cloud. Her thoughts circle endlessly around Kore—and the hope she clings to like breath.

Footsteps.

Soft, hesitant, barely audible above the slow drip of water.

She stirs. The motion is a quiet rebellion, a labor that rips through her chest like fire. She forces herself upright, each breath shallow, tight.

A figure appears at the cell door.

Ingus.

His face is pale, his brow slick with sweat. His hands tremble as they grip the bars.

"I tried," he whispers. The words shake with guilt. "I tried, Edith."

Her lips twist into a bitter smile. "Spare me thy apologies," she croaks. Her voice is cracked but still carries defiance. "It is only a matter of time. Kore will return with the antidote. She will not fail."

Ingus shifts uncomfortably, his eyes darting toward the corners of the dungeon. "How canst thou be so sure?" he murmurs. "She ventures into the Voidspire Gateways. Among the Kelxsiar. Places no mortal dares walk."

"She knows the paths," Edith answers, her tone sharpening despite her withering strength. "She hath seen the Kelxsiar use them. Studied their movements. With every battle, she learns. With every escape, she remembers."

She leans back against the cold wall, her breath ragged. "She will return. She must."

Suddenly, a groan escapes her lips.

Her hand flies to her chest as veins ripple dark across her skin—black, branching tendrils creeping over her golden form. Her divine glow dims further, eyes bloodshot, streaked with crimson. Her body, once radiant, now looks caught between realms—part celestial, part withering mortal.

"What… what is happening to me?" she gasps.

Ingus falters, the words catching in his throat. "You're dying," he says finally, and the words drop like stone into silence. "Whatever thou art… this world rejects it. It poisons thee. Drags thee down into mortality."

Edith turns her head, slowly. Her dimming eyes fix on him. "And what of thee?" she asks, her voice low but laced with venom. "Why dost thou still walk free? Why hast thou not been chained beside me?"

"The town needs my services," he replies stiffly, but fear cracks his voice. "I have not been spared completely."

He pulls back his sleeve. Faint bruises mar his pale skin.

"They punish me in… other ways."

Edith laughs, dry and bitter. It ends in a cough of pain. "Even cowards find ways to survive."

Ingus flinches. Shame flickers in his eyes. "And what of thy sister?" he asks, desperate now. "How canst thou trust she will find this cure?"

Edith's voice lowers, soft but burning with quiet intensity. "Because she hath no choice. We are all we have left. And Kore…"

She pauses.

Her voice falters for the first time, but then it returns, steady, steel-edged. "She knows what's at stake. She will not let me die."

The words hang in the stillness like a prayer spoken to no one.

Above them, the muffled noise of the townsfolk continues—a world moving on without them. But here in the cell, surrounded by rot and silence, Edith clings to life. Her body betrays her, but her spirit refuses to yield.

In the shadows, she waits—for her sister, for

salvation, for vengeance.

PAR

The air in Voidspire Yard hangs thick with ash and the acrid tang of scorched metal, clinging to Kore's skin despite the heavy coating of black oil she smears across herself. The vivid crimson hue of her body—once a glaring mark of her cursed lineage—is now hidden beneath a glistening sheen of darkness. She crouches low to the cracked earth, her breath shallow, her golden eyes scanning the dead expanse ahead.

The ruins stretch endlessly, interrupted only by jagged rock formations and clusters of twisted steel—remnants of a war long turned to dust. Once, she was forged into a hunter by the Kelxsiar, trained to kill without hesitation. But now, every scar, every sharpened instinct, turns against them.

Ahead looms a massive, crumbling structure—the Firmament Temple.

It rises from the wasteland like the skeletal husk of a forgotten god. Once, this place held sacred purpose: a haven for Par warriors, where they confessed their doubts and drew strength from their faith. But now, its spires jut skyward like broken fingers clawing at a blood-colored sky. The walls are fractured, etched with violence. No blessings remain. The Vast Sea has long abandoned this ground. It is hollow now. Desecrated. Forsaken.

Kore presses her body to the earth, sliding into a prone position. Her blackened form blends seamlessly with the shadows. Beyond the barbed-wire fences, Kelxsiar rovers prowl the perimeter—nightmares made flesh and alloy. Their twisted forms are part-organic, part-machine, plates of liquid metal shifting over muscle and bone. Sickly green cores pulse at their centers, beating like corrupted hearts, casting pale light across the blood-stained ground.

She watches them closely.

Their movements are mechanical—precise, efficient—but above all, predictable. That is their flaw. And she will exploit it.

The sky begins to brighten. The blood-red sun breaches the horizon, bathing the realm in its eerie glow. Kore's oil-covered skin will betray her soon—its sheen a beacon in the light.

There is no more time.

She draws a breath through her teeth and bolts forward. Her legs pump with unholy speed, barely brushing the earth as she sprints toward the fence.

Then—

The shadows shift.

Kore stops cold, instincts screaming. The ground ripples beneath her feet, darkness pooling like liquid tar. A rover steps from the void, its tendrils snapping through the air like whips. It lunges.

The impact slams her mid-sprint, tendrils coiling around her waist. She's driven into the dirt, the air forced from her lungs. The rover looms, shrieking—a hideous blend of metal and primal rage. Its sound shakes the earth.

Kore's eyes blacken. Her body responds with instinctual fury. With a sharp crack, her claws extend—curved, gleaming obsidian blades. She roars, her voice thick with rage and heartbreak, and drives her claws into the rover's chest.

The machine thrashes, its tendrils slashing her arms and tearing at her face, but she holds. Her claws shred through its plating, fingers curling around its core. With a brutal squeeze, she crushes it. The glow dies. The rover twitches once, then goes still.

Kore shoves the husk aside and staggers upright, chest heaving. Her eyes flick across the horizon.

No others come.

Only the faint hum of Kelxsiar machinery hums in the distance.

"They only left one," she mutters, suspicion

curling in her gut. "Why guard a temple with a single sentry?"

She glances at the fence, then vaults over it in a clean leap. Her boots land heavy on cracked stone—but her motion is quiet, controlled.

Inside, the temple reeks of decay. The air is heavy, stagnant with dust and mold. The grand atrium yawns before her, once majestic, now a desecrated crypt. Massive columns rise like sentinels, but their carved murals are faded—images of Par warriors kneeling in prayer before the Vast Sea, now worn and ghostlike.

Her footsteps echo softly as she moves toward the altar.

She knows the Kelxsiar's love of ambush.

Every shadow is suspect.

But when she reaches the altar, she halts—eyes wide.

A mountain of wreckage rises before her. Void-spire Engines—once divine instruments of inter-dimensional travel—now lie broken and forgotten. Their cores, long dark, are lifeless husks of what was once salvation.

Her chest tightens.

"Freedom is where they failed us," she whispers bitterly, her voice low with fury.

She climbs the pile, claws scraping over rusted metal. The structure shifts under her weight, groaning like a wounded beast. Near the top, a faint blue glow pulses through the debris.

One engine lives.

She drops beside it, pries open its access hatch, and exposes a control panel lit by flickering runes. Her fingers hover.

Then—

A beam of light shoots from the panel, striking her eyes.

She gasps, paralyzed as the world turns white.

A voice floods her mind—distorted, mechanical, yet laced with reverence. It echoes like a divine echo from beyond time.

> *"Attention to the divine Par race. In the event of the kingdom's fall, these engines house the locations of all Par beings and outposts distributed across the universe. Use this knowledge to find refuge amongst the millions of new worlds. Conquer them. Rule them."*

The voice vanishes.

The engine beeps once.

Then silence.

Kore stumbles back, clutching her head. Pain surges through her skull—sharp, searing. The knowledge carves itself into her mind. She can see every outpost, every coordinate. The map of survival—branded into her consciousness like a curse.

She drops to her knees, opens the engine's lower compartment, and finds a scroll tucked inside.

Hands trembling, she unrolls it.

A registry of bloodlines.

Her eyes scan the names—her father's… her mother's… Edith's…

But her name is not there.

The scroll falls from her grip. It lands with a soft, final *thud*.

Black tears spill from her eyes. They trail down her cheeks, scalding her crimson skin like acid.

"Why do you hate me?!" she screams, her voice reverberating through the empty temple.

The silence answers with movement.

The shadows stir.

Kelxsiar emerge—shimmering, grotesque, like phantoms born of oil and steel. One steps forward, voice guttural, distorted.

"Detain the escapee."

But Kore does not move.

She remains kneeling, head bowed, claws limp at her sides. She does not raise a hand in defiance.

This time, she does not fight.

She surrenders—not to them, but to the deeper wound inside her.

The wound of being forsaken.

4

A Lesser Evil

Bethany's wings ache as though forged from lead, each beat heavier than the last. She has soared for what feels like an eternity, the heavens stretching endlessly above while the ocean below whispers dark secrets to the wind. A faint memory of the maps engraved in her mind reassures her that an outpost lies ahead—an outpost said to harbor the Par minerals, the only hope of fashioning a cure for Edith. Her sister's fragile body struggles against the weight of this realm's cruel air, like a bird ensnared in a tempest. The chance of success is slim, but Bethany has wagered Edith's life on thinner odds before. She would sacrifice the world itself if it meant saving her kin.

The island looms on the horizon—abrupt, stark, veiled in shadows cast by an overcast sky. Jagged peaks pierce the heavens, their roots swallowed by a labyrinth of primeval forest. Bethany tilts her wings, her body carving through the air as she begins her descent. The trees stretch toward her like skeletal hands, their branches whispering secrets in the ancient tongues of nature. She spins into a wide glide, her wings folding slightly to catch the updraft. As she pierces the canopy, a sudden gust of wind rips through the underbrush, scattering leaves and exposing the skeletal remains of creatures long forgotten. The land greets her with silence—a silence that hangs thick, as if riddled with unseen eyes.

Her boots hit the mossy earth, and the forest seems to recoil. The air here is dense, soured with foreboding. Each step she takes crushes the underbrush beneath her, the sound echoing like brittle bones snapping beneath weight. She presses forward, every shadow a potential threat, every sound a harbinger of some unseen doom. Her pulse quickens when a sudden noise fractures the stillness—a muffled gasp, followed by the guttural snarl of something not quite of this world.

Bethany moves swiftly but silently, her breath shallow, her hand closing around the hilt of the dagger sheathed at her side. The forest thickens, as though conspiring to hold her back, but she pushes through, driven by the urgency of the sound—by instinct and desperation.

What she finds is a nightmare given flesh.

A Kelxsiar Hunter looms over its prey, its monstrous form flickering in and out of reality like a candle in the wind. Its crimson eyes burn like coals. Its teeth, long and glistening, drip saliva that sizzles as it hits the moss, as if laced with acid. Under its massive paw lies a luminous figure, her body broken and trembling. The creature has pinned her down, its claws sunken deep into her translucent skin, which pulses faintly with veins of glowing light. Her gossamer-thin wings twitch feebly beneath the crushing weight, struggling to free themselves. Her matted hair, streaked with what appears to be blood—not red, but a stark and unnatural white—pools beneath her and soaks into the soil like spilled moonlight.

Bethany's eyes widen. Her breath catches in her throat. She has no certainty if this creature—or the glowing being beneath it—has anything to do with the outpost she seeks. But leaving without answers is not an option.

Her muscles tense as she inhales deeply, her mind sharpening like a honed blade.

"Loathe I am to make thy acquaintance, foul thing," she mutters under her breath before launching forward.

Bethany hurls herself into the fray, her wings snapping open with a deafening crack. She spins mid-air, curling her body and slamming her full weight into the beast's skull. The Hunter roars, staggering as it releases its prey. The glowing woman scrambles backward, her wings dragging through the dirt, her ragged breaths trembling through the trees.

Bethany hits the ground hard, rolls, and rises fluidly, dagger drawn. The beast recovers with stunning speed, shaking its massive head like a wild bull. Its fiery eyes lock onto her. A guttural growl wells deep in its chest before it lunges, jaws snapping just inches from her face.

She twists, slashing upward—but the creature vanishes, phasing out just before her blade can connect. It reappears behind her with a low snarl, its claws tearing through the back of her tunic and raking across her skin. Bethany cries out, pain bursting through her nerves as her wings flare wide, knocking the Hunter backward with the force of their unfurling.

The beast roars and charges again, slamming her to the ground, pinning her beneath its tremendous bulk. Its breath washes over her like a rotting wind, the stench of sulfur and decay turning her stomach. Its jaws widen, teeth gleaming inches from her throat.

Bethany struggles, her strength faltering beneath its crushing weight.

Then—

A thunderous crack splits the air. The Hunter's skull erupts in a geyser of blue-black gore, the viscous fluid showering her face and chest. The beast's body collapses lifeless atop her.

Gasping, Bethany shoves the corpse off. She sits up, wiping blood from her eyes, blinking through the blur.

Standing just beyond the carcass is the glowing woman. Her arm is outstretched, fingers still smoking with residual energy. Wisps of ghostly flame ripple from her palm, dissipating into the air.

"Thou couldst not have done that sooner?" Bethany demands, her voice sharp and breathless with frustration.

"I had need to gather mine strength," the woman replies evenly, though her tone is laced with exhaustion. Her accent is strange, every word laced with the cadence of a world not born of Earth.

Bethany rises, wary, her gaze narrowing. "What art thou? Speak plainly."

"I am Nerl," the woman says, her glowing eyes locking with Bethany's. "We hail from the Leprine Realm. My name is Vestegia."

Bethany's brow furrows. The name stirs no recognition, but the race does. "The Par hath laid waste to thy kind," she says, her voice gentler now. "I have seen thy kin enslaved. Wings clipped. Spirits crushed."

Vestegia's jaw tightens. Her eyes burn with restrained rage. "Thou speakest truth, though it wounds me to hear it. We fled. We rewrote the coordinates of the Voidspire Engines. That is how we found these scattered outposts."

Bethany steps forward. Her voice is low, urgent. "Then thou hast the knowledge I seek. I need Par minerals. I need them to save my sister. Wilt thou help me?"

Vestegia's form flickers, her glow dimming momentarily as she studies Bethany. Suspicion flares in her eyes. "Why should I help thee? Thy kind hath brought naught but ruin upon mine own."

Bethany does not flinch. She steps even closer, voice sharp as steel. "Look upon me, Nerl. I am no ally to the Par. They cast me out. Branded me traitor. My father—their leader—fell by my hand. That beast hunted thee as it hunts me. Whether thou likest it or not, our fates are now entwined."

Vestegia hesitates. Her light pulses with tension, then softens. At last, she nods once.

"Very well. Come—I shall show thee the way. But heed my words—trust between us will not come easily."

Bethany exhales, her shoulders relaxing. Her grip loosens on the dagger.

"I ask not for trust," she says. "Only thy aid."

The air grows colder as Bethany and Vestegia descend into the deepening woods. Shadows braid themselves through the dying rays of light, stretching long and ominous across the gnarled roots that jut from the earth like skeletal fingers clawing toward the surface. Each step forward invites a thicker, more unnerving silence—broken only by the brittle crunch of leaves underfoot. The canopy above weaves tighter with every stride, unnaturally dense, as though the very forest resents their presence. Darkness gathers there like breath held too long, pressing heavily on Bethany's wings.

"Is this the outpost?" Bethany asks, her voice steady though unease scratches at her thoughts.

"The outpost lieth far from here," Vestegia replies, her tone distant, dipped in something like mourning.

"Lieth? Speak plain," Bethany presses, eyeing her warily. "What dost thou mean?"

Vestegia's glow dims as she slows her pace. "The outpost was razed," she says. "After we fled, the Kelxsiar scoured its bones, ensuring naught remained to stake thy people's claim upon these woods."

Bethany stops cold. Her feathers ruffle with restrained tension, eyes narrowing. "Then where dost thou lead me?"

Vestegia turns, her luminous gaze locking onto Bethany's. "Home."

Before Bethany can speak again, the ground beneath them groans—a dreadful, resonant sound like the earth itself protesting their intrusion. A jagged crevice tears open with a deafening crack, revealing a stone staircase that spirals deep into the earth. From within the rift, faint bioluminescent light spills outward, casting ghostly blue hues that shimmer over the forest floor like moonlit mist.

Bethany tenses, her wings twitching instinctively. Suspicion narrows her eyes as she looks to Vestegia. "This… this is thy home?"

Vestegia nods solemnly. "'Tis all we have left."

Against every instinct shouting to turn back, Bethany follows. As they descend, the air thickens—damp, cloying, and sour with the scent of moss and slow decay. Beneath it lingers something sharper, metallic and strange, like burnt ozone after a storm. The stone gives way to walls of root and earth, twisted into living architecture that pulses faintly with internal light, as though the passage itself breathes.

They emerge into a vast chamber—an underground sanctuary carved by time and sorrow. It glows with quiet life. Dozens of Nerl beings move within, their translucent skin glimmering in soft waves of green and gold. Their movements are elegant, but fatigued. Every gesture betrays the weight of survival worn threadbare.

"Only a remnant of us remain," Vestegia says quietly, her eyes drifting over her people. They move among strange, otherworldly flora—luminescent plants that radiate a pale, mournful glow. Wands made from twisted vine and crystal bones rest in their hands, weapons of beauty and mourning.

Bethany's eyes land on a bed of flowers humming with low, ethereal resonance. Their petals ripple with ancient magic, and within their design she recognizes something terrible—an echo of her father's war spoils. She had seen them before, trophies in his halls. The sight now churns her stomach with old fury and newer shame.

"What is that?" a deep voice growls from the shadows.

Bethany turns sharply. A towering Nerl steps into view, his frame massive, wrapped in a flowing mantle of woven root and bark. His eyes, dark and cutting, fix on her with immediate disdain.

"'Tis a Par Realmer," Vestegia answers quickly.

"I know what she is," he snaps. "What I demand is why she treads here, among us."

"Lypar," Vestegia begins, her voice pleading, "she hath saved my life. She is not—"

"Not what?" he interrupts, advancing with coiled

menace. "A predator? A viper come to slither in our den? Hast thou so quickly forgotten what her kind hath wrought?"

"I am no viper," Bethany declares, stepping forward without hesitation. Her voice slices through the tension, calm and lethal. "Were I here to slay thee, I would have drawn my sword ere now."

Lypar's eyes narrow. His aura looms like a storm ready to break. "And were we to wish thy death," he growls, "thou wouldst never draw breath again."

The cavern stills. All movement halts as the others watch the exchange with wary silence. The air thickens, the moment suspended like a blade poised mid-drop. Bethany's wings twitch at her back, muscles taut, her instinct to strike battling the wisdom to hold her ground.

"She hath earned our aid," Vestegia says, her voice trembling, but firm with conviction. "She risked all to save me."

Lypar's sneer deepens. He eyes Bethany like a sickness in need of quarantine. "Very well," he mutters, his voice low and dangerous. "But mark me, Par. My mercy is thin—and my patience, thinner still."

With a sharp motion, he grabs a vial from a Nerl crouched beside the glowing flora. The liquid within shimmers like molten starlight, a rare and sacred remedy.

"Take this, and begone," Lypar commands, thrusting it toward Bethany. "And know this—thou art not welcome here again."

Bethany takes the vial, her grip steady though her eyes remain locked on his. "I seek no quarrel," she says coolly. "My purpose is mine own. I will trouble thee no further."

Lypar's gaze darkens, his voice thick with resentment. "Thy kind hath brought only ruin. Thy father's blood runs in thy veins still—and I shall never forget the shadow he casteth over our kind."

Bethany's jaw tightens. Her wings rustle, feathers trembling at the edge of fury. "My father is ash," she says. "His deeds, cursed even in my own heart. Do not mistake me for the monster who bore me."

Lypar says nothing. His silence is a blade unsheathed.

Bethany turns, brushing past the cavern wall as she walks with measured restraint. The moment she reaches the surface, she does not hesitate.

She takes flight.

The cool air lashes against her skin as she rises into the night sky. The wind howls around her like a lament, and with every powerful stroke of her wings, she puts greater distance between herself and the buried sanctuary below. The chill of the heavens clears her lungs. The ghosts of her father's legacy gnaw at her heels, but she does not look back.

Far below, in the stillness of the cavern, Vestegia lingers beneath Lypar's simmering gaze.

"Thou hast brought a serpent among us," he says, voice like frost.

"And yet," Vestegia replies softly, "she saved my life."

"She may yet bring ruin upon us," Lypar mutters, his jaw tight.

"She is not her father," Vestegia insists, the words barely above a whisper.

Lypar's eyes remain fixed on the path Bethany had taken. "Perhaps," he concedes at last. "But even the smallest ember… may yet reignite a wildfire."

Bethany's flight from the outpost is swift and frantic, her crimson wings slicing through the night like jagged shadows cutting across a dark canvas. The air hangs heavy with the dampness of an impending storm, clinging to her skin, chilling her bones. Her thoughts spiral as she flies. She has just faced enemies born of her own father's blood-feud—his most despised foes—and from their reluctant hands, she has secured salvation for her sister, Edith. The irony cuts deep, a blade turned inward and twisted slow.

The Nerls gave her the cure. A way to restore her sister's dwindling divinity. But they did so with venom in their eyes and bitterness on their tongues. Still, Bethany bears them no resentment. How could she? Not when her only aim is to save Edith. Not when she's lived a life of exile, while her sister walked beneath a golden sky, untouched by the scars their parents left behind.

Edith inherited grace. Untainted, undeserved grace—bestowed freely, almost thoughtlessly. A purity Bethany will never know. Her wings may carry her through the heavens, but her soul crawls through the mire. She envies nothing. She regrets everything.

Her flight stutters.

Memories claw at her like hands from the grave. The shrieks of the wounded. The stench of blood. The desperate cry of a girl she left behind.

Kamilah.

The slave girl. Fragile. Mistreated. Broken beneath the weight of cruel hands and chains. Bethany had seen her—seen the suffering carved into her bones—and yet she left. Could she have escaped? Bethany *wants* to believe so. But something vile twists in her gut, telling her otherwise.

She must know. She *must* see.

Her descent into the woods is silent as shadow, her body veiled by the thick canopy above. Darkness here is absolute—consuming, unyielding. The world disappears into void. Only the faint moonlight filtering through the treetops gives her form any shape. Her crimson skin shimmers beneath it, but it is her eyes—those burning, spectral red eyes—that shine brightest, casting their glow like twin beacons in the black.

She glides low over dew-kissed grass, silent as death, moving toward the pit—*that* pit—where Kamilah had been shackled like an animal.

The air reeks of damp earth and old blood. The remnants of cruelty still stain this place, thick as tar. Bethany crouches beside the pit, her clawed hands brushing over the rusted iron chains, now broken and cold.

They're empty.

Relief flickers in her chest. But it doesn't last.

Where is she?

Did she escape? Or did they move her—drag her to a darker fate?

Bethany prowls forward, silent and predatory. Her wings fold tightly against her back as she slips like a wraith through the camp. Every step is deliberate. Every breath is shallow. The compound lies in ruin, abandoned but not forgotten. Wind weaves through the tattered remnants of banners that once heralded the soldiers' dominion. Now, they are just echoes.

She searches the barracks. The blood-stained torture chambers. The open, barren fields where ash still clings to the soil. She checks every crumbling corner of this desolate place.

But Kamilah is nowhere.

Her heart begins to sink, the weight unbearable. Her wings unfurl slightly, ready to depart, to return to Edith with the vial—and with failure.

Then she sees it.

A silhouette—strange, suspended—just beyond the glow of her gaze, hanging beneath the boughs of a massive oak tree.

Her steps slow, each one heavier than the last. Her chest tightens as the shape becomes clearer.

It's familiar.

Horribly familiar.

And wrong.

There, dangling from the gnarled branches, is Kamilah.

Bethany freezes. Her breath catches in her throat. The world blurs. A strange ringing floods her ears as the full, unbearable horror sets in.

Kamilah's body swings gently, lifeless, moved only by the breeze. Her arms hang twisted at unnatural angles. Her face is swollen and shattered, bloodied beyond recognition. The rope around her neck bites deep into her flesh. Crude symbols—carved into her torso—mark her like a cursed offering, a grotesque final act of hatred.

"No..." Bethany breathes, the word a ghost on

her lips.

Her knees buckle. She collapses into the earth, trembling, her claws digging into the soil as she stares. "No!"

Her scream tears from her throat, jagged and raw, the cry of something sacred being broken. The sound echoes across the trees, shaking the branches, startling birds from their roosts. The forest itself seems to recoil.

Bethany staggers upright. Her fists clench. Her claws pierce her own palms. Grief ignites into something far more violent.

Rage.

The air around her thickens. It shimmers. It crackles with barely contained power.

"Kamilah..." she whispers, reaching toward the hanging body, her hand trembling with guilt and rage. "I should have saved thee. I should have—"

Her voice fails her. Her fury consumes it.

With a feral roar, she hurls herself skyward. Her wings snap open with a thunderous *crack*, launching her into the heavens like a living projectile. The shock wave blasts outward, rattling the trees and cracking branches as she ascends with a fury unmatched.

Thunder answers her.

The skies roll and weep.

Rain begins to pour—hard and fast—washing

over the blood-soaked earth and the horror left beneath the oak.

Bethany vanishes into the storm, the heavens reflecting the war now raging in her heart.

5

Them?

A thunderous crash shatters the silence of the cell, jolting Edith from the abyss of her fevered agony. She barely stirs. Her once-golden skin now wears the pallor of death, veins blackened with the sickness that gnaws at her from within. A sickness that twists her divine ichor—the sacred gold of her blood—into something foul. Mortal. Weak.

The air thickens around her, steeped in damp rot. The stench of old death clings to the stone walls like a lingering curse that time itself refuses to cleanse.

The cell door shrieks open.

A soldier looms in the threshold, his silhouette jagged against the flickering torchlight. Malice glints in his eyes—the kind of cruelty men wield like divine right when they believe themselves chosen. Justified. Holy.

"Get up, whore!" he snarls, his voice a venom-laced whip. He punctuates the command with a savage kick to the cot's rotting wood.

Edith doesn't move. Her body is a collapsing ruin, fever devouring her bones from the inside out. She pulls in a breath through cracked lips—slow, painful, each inhalation a war.

"I cannot," she rasps, her voice barely more than a ghost clinging to the air.

The soldier scoffs. "You will."

The boot crashes down again—harder this time—slamming into her stomach with brute force. A guttural cry spills from her lips. She curls reflexively, her body folding inward, trembling under pain that would have once meant nothing to her.

"Move, witch!" he barks. "Your kind's excuses are worth naught but spit."

A voice calls from the corridor beyond. "Drag her if you must!"

The order is all the soldier needs. Rough hands seize her fragile body, yanking her off the cot. She hits the floor with a sickening thud, stone grating against her skin. Jagged edges carve fresh wounds into arms already battered and bruised beyond recognition.

There is no fight left in her.

The divine fire that once danced in her veins has

withered to smoke and ash.

He drags her without care. Her limbs trail behind like broken branches, her body leaving a faint trail of blood and filth across the stone floor. As they cross the arched threshold into the courtyard, she squeezes her eyes shut against the light.

Then—agony.

Daylight stabs into her eyes, as merciless as the men who seek her end. Even through her delirium, she hears them—murmuring voices, shuffling feet. A crowd gathers.

A noose sways before her. It hangs like a patient viper, coiled and waiting.

Rough hands wrench her upright, dragging her onto the wooden platform. The boards groan beneath her weight. A coarse rope bites into her wrists, binding them tightly behind her back. She sways on unsteady legs, the world a haze of heat and pain.

Through blurred vision, she sees the faces. A sea of them. Men, women, even children—watching with bated breath. Some stare with smug satisfaction. Others look hungry, their eyes devouring every tremor of her suffering.

A figure steps forward—draped in the black robes of the clergy. The village priest. A gaunt man with hollow eyes and the voice of God sharpened into a blade.

"It has come to our attention that thou hath stolen the name of a dead woman," he declares, every syllable steeped in disdain. "And so, this wicked creature—this unholy thing whose true name remains unknown—shall suffer the same fate. Ye have been found guilty of consorting with devils, of conjuring witchcraft, and for these sins, thou shalt hang."

Edith's breath rattles in her throat. Her body trembles with violent shivers, barely able to remain upright. Pain pierces her, relentless and merciless—but the priest's words barely register.

She knew this would come. From the moment her body failed her, she accepted her fate.

Perhaps… death is a mercy.

She exhales shallowly, her gaze drifting down to the wooden planks beneath her bare feet. She sees the trapdoor lines—thin slashes in the wood, waiting to open beneath her and welcome her into the abyss.

The priest's voice grows distant. "Have ye any last words?"

She does not speak.

Instead, she lifts her head and meets his gaze. Her eyes, though sunken and rimmed with shadows, hold a flicker of defiance—a dim, dying ember against the vast dark.

"May God have mercy on thy damned soul."

The executioner pulls the lever.

A sharp crack splits the air as the trapdoor gives way. The noose yanks upward.

But in that same instant—

A blur. A shadow. A whisper of wings.

A flash of steel cuts through the noose mid-air.

Edith falls forward, the sudden drop jarring her senses. Her body slams into the wooden structure before crashing hard onto the ground below. Pain detonates in her chest. The world spins wildly as she gasps for breath, her lungs sucking in precious air.

Above her, something looms.

Massive, oil-slicked wings unfurl like a thunderhead sweeping across the sky. Their inky feathers devour the light. The air thickens, charged with an ancient, unnatural presence. The scent of burning metal and rot floods Edith's lungs.

Bethany.

She stands before the execution platform, her posture rigid, her presence a storm barely restrained. Her crimson skin glistens beneath the sun's brutal glare. Black claws twitch at her sides, eager, impatient. But it's her eyes—those burning, seething red eyes—that freeze every soul that dares to look.

The priest recoils. His face twists in horror.

"This is what ye wished for, is it not?" Bethany

asks, her voice calm as a tomb, yet carrying the weight of a coming cataclysm. "Ye sought to witness the damnation of a soul, yet could not wait for Heaven's judgment. Very well."

The glow in her eyes intensifies, smoldering like coals about to erupt into wildfire.

"Behold."

Terror ripples through the crowd. Murmurs erupt. Murmurs become gasps. Gasps become screams.

"Bethany..." Edith croaks. Her voice is raw, scraped thin.

Bethany glances down. For the first time, her lips curl—not in cruelty, nor in kindness, but something unreadable. Ancient.

"There is no need for the falsehood any longer," she says. "Nor is there reason to pretend we are as weak as those who surround us."

From within her robes, she withdraws a vial.

It shimmers—golden, luminous. Divine blood. Pure. Untainted. A cure.

"Drink, sister. Regain thy strength."

Her voice drops lower—darker. Something monstrous curls beneath the surface. Her jaw clenches. From her temples, jagged horns begin to emerge, twisting like ancient roots breaking through sacred ground. The air crackles with energy. The very earth beneath her darkens.

Edith stares, her pulse thundering.

This is not Bethany.

This is Kore.

Kore, the forsaken. Kore, the cursed. Kore, the demon of Par.

And as Edith lifts the vial to her trembling lips, a cold certainty settles into her bones.

Before this night ends, the village will drown in screams.

Edith's breath wavered as consciousness crept back into her bones. The weight of sickness that once devoured her from within had vanished, replaced by a vigor she had not felt in what seemed an eternity. Her skin, once marred by the curse of mortality, had regained its divine glow—smooth and unbroken as polished gold. The light of her celestial eyes flickered back to life, casting an ethereal luminance upon the blood-stained earth. And her hair—once dulled and knotted by sickness—now flowed like molten light, silken strands cascading over her shoulders.

She rose, her every sinew reborn with celestial strength. Her wings, grand and unyielding, unfurled behind her in a flourish of divine splendor, their brilliant plumage casting rippling shadows across the desecrated land. But something was wrong. Something beyond the restoration of her form.

A fetid stench clung to the air, thick as rotting flesh. Her bare feet found purchase upon ground slick with coagulating blood. Edith staggered, her mind struggling to grasp the carnage laid before her. Bodies, eviscerated and torn asunder, littered the earth in grotesque sculptures of agony. Faces frozen in terror stared blindly into the heavens, their throats gaping red as if they had begged for mercy in their last breath. Limbs were strewn like discarded remnants of a butcher's table. The ichor pooled, seeping into the soil, staining it with the final remnants of human prayers unanswered.

A slow tremor overtook her hands. "Dear sister… what hast thou done?"

A gust of wind whispered through the silence, heralding the descent of a shadowed figure. Bethany dropped from the sky with effortless grace, her landing gentle, yet her presence heavier than the weight of the dead. Her wings—charred black as an oil-drenched night—folded against her back. Her feet disturbed the blood, yet it did not seem to cling to her.

"I have done unto them as they meant to do unto thee," Bethany said, her voice cold as a grave unblessed.

Edith's breath hitched. "Nay, sister… this is not our way."

Bethany scoffed, stepping over a corpse with

detached indifference. "Thou speakest as though we were made for peace." She turned her gaze upon Edith, eyes burning like dying embers in a pit of smoldering ruin. "We were not. We are born to rule, to crush, to cleanse this wretched world with fire and fury. Dost thou not feel it? The hunger? The power?"

Edith shook her head, gripping her own arms as if to keep herself from shattering. "We fled Par to escape such darkness."

Bethany took another step forward. "Par, Earth-Void—it matters not. The weak will always fall to the strong."

Edith's gaze swept across the slaughter, the bodies stacked in their silent testimony. She turned to Bethany, pleading, but her voice was barely above a whisper. "What hast thou done…?"

Bethany met her gaze, unflinching. "What needed be done."

Her voice was a blade, slicing through whatever remnants of warmth remained between them. Edith's trembling hand reached for her, but the moment her fingers brushed Bethany's arm, her sister recoiled, her lips curling into a sneer.

"Thou pitiest them, dost thou not?" Bethany's expression twisted with contempt. "These cattle? These filth-ridden mongrels who would see thee burn?"

Edith's heart pounded. "This is not thee, Bethany—" She hesitated, the name tasting foreign on her tongue. "Nay… thou art not Bethany. Thou art Kore."

Bethany's smile was slow, eerie. "Ah. So at last, thou speakest truth."

She took a deliberate step forward, and instinctively, Edith stepped back.

"Thou wouldst know, wouldst thou not? The favored daughter. The golden child," Bethany mused, her voice thick with something sinister. "Thy blood is pure. Thine inheritance divine. And yet… thou thinkest me of the same flesh?"

Edith frowned. "What speakest thou of?"

Bethany's wings twitched. "Thou takest me for a fool? How long, I wonder, didst thou believe me blind? Didst thou think I knew not? Thou wouldst play me for one of these frail beasts… but I am no fool."

Edith swallowed, uncertainty gripping her. "Sister, I—"

"Silence!" Bethany's voice cracked like thunder. "Dost thou not see? Thou hast turned to weakness. Thy sickness made thee no better than they who caged thee, spat upon thee. Thou wert to be divine, yet here thou art, trembling like a frightened doe. Our father wouldst cast thee out for this."

Edith's blood ran cold. "Our father—"

Bethany's gaze darkened. "Thine. Not mine."

A shadow passed over Edith's face. "Nay… nay, that is false."

"He hath said otherwise," Bethany hissed.

For a moment, silence loomed between them, broken only by the distant caw of ravens circling above, drawn to the feast of the dead.

Edith swallowed down her dread. "We must leave this place. We must find another land to dwell."

Bethany did not answer. Instead, she turned, her wings extending to their fullest, their inky expanse blotting out the feeble morning light.

Without another word, she launched herself skyward, the wind of her departure scattering the bloodied leaves below.

Edith stood frozen, her breath unsteady, her heart heavy with a fear that no longer belonged to the mortals she once pitied.

It belonged to her.

* * *

At This Moment

Edith trembled as she forced herself upright, her entire body trembling beneath the strain. Her wings twitched violently in their ruined state, convulsing as they struggled to mend fractured bones and torn tendons. Blood seeped from jagged breaks, slicking her skin with its ethereal, celestial hue. A tremor of pain rippled through her core, but she swallowed it down with effort, lifting her eyes to meet the malevolent glow burning within her sister's gaze.

Bethany stood in still defiance, her presence unnervingly composed yet dripping with menace. Her bare feet pressed into the ruined earth, toes curling slightly in the dirt as if she drew strength from the decay. The air around her thickened, laden with malice that coiled like smoke. Her lips curled, just barely—an amused sneer flickering within her crimson-lit stare like a cruel ember threatening to catch.

"Beneath me," Bethany hissed, her voice a rasp, raw with contempt and scorched by years of buried scorn. Her arm jerked outward, and from the torn flesh of her back, blackened sinew and muscle writhed. Twisting together with grotesque preci- sion, they birthed leathery wings—new, unnatural things of horror and hatred. With a sudden, vicious motion, she swung her arm and hurled a blade of sharpened bone toward Edith.

Edith twisted back on instinct alone, her battered form screaming in protest. She narrowly avoided the full blow, but a thin gash opened along her cheek, the near-miss branding her with searing pain. The wound stung, blood warm against the chill of the night.

"Thou art weak," Bethany snarled, her wings flexing behind her like a grotesque shroud. Their monstrous length blotted out the fractured moon above, casting her silhouette like a demon's over the battlefield. "Yet *I* was cast out? Nay. The feeble should be discarded like carrion."

With a shriek of fury, Edith lunged forward, her battered fists swinging in raw defiance. Her form, broken but unyielding, moved on pure will. But Bethany's reflexes were honed by hatred and sharpened by divine wrath. She caught Edith's wrist mid-strike with terrifying ease, her fingers curling around the fragile bone—

Snap.

A sickening crack echoed in the air. Edith gasped, a strangled cry caught in her throat as white-hot agony bloomed through her arm. Her vision blurred, her strength faltering. Bethany's lips stretched wide into something monstrous, her

teeth bared in a grin of bloodthirsty delight, her
eyes wild with spite.

"Thy father. Thy mother!" Bethany screamed,
her voice cracking under the weight of betrayal,
thick with ancient grief. Hatred clawed its way up
her throat, raw and festering. "Did they not love
thee more? Did they not shield thee whilst *I* was
cast unto the wolves?"

She rose into the air, wind howling violently
around her, echoing like a chorus of wailing spirits
mourning the ruin of sisterhood. Then, with
terrifying velocity, she plummeted—fists wreathed
in unholy force. Her strike came like a comet
crashing from heaven, hammering Edith down
into the soil. The ground buckled and cracked
beneath the blow, forming a crater beneath their
feet.

Edith choked on blood, her limbs convulsing, her
lungs fighting against the crushing weight of her
sister's fury. The world spun in crimson and black
as her vision dimmed at the edges.

Bethany loomed above her, chest heaving, eyes
wild and shining with a storm of emotions. Within
that fury flickered something else—a conflict, a
memory, a glimpse of what once was. A candle's
flicker fighting a hurricane.

"Please," Edith rasped, her voice barely more than
a breath, ragged and broken.

Bethany hesitated.

For the briefest moment, her expression shifted. Her gaze wavered, and her lips parted—not with rage, but sorrow. That moment, a fleeting echo of the sister she had once been, hovered in the air like a dying star.

Then, the storm within her surged again.

"Nay," Bethany whispered, her tone laced with finality and regret. She stepped back, wings spreading wide. "Thou hast chosen thy side, Edith."

With a powerful beat of her wings, she ascended. The heavens seemed to tremble in her wake as she vanished into the abyss of the night. Her departure left the air dense with dread, as though the sky itself mourned.

Edith longed to follow, to call her back from the madness threatening to consume her soul. But even as her heart surged forward, her body remained grounded in grim truth—she could not win. Not now. Bethany had become something else, something unholy, something far beyond even Edith's worst fears.

With a ragged grunt, she pushed herself upright once more. Her wings dragged behind her, smeared in divine blood that dripped like ink from broken quills. Gritting her teeth, she reached for the shattered joints, forcing bone back into alignment with guttural, agonized groans.

Then—

A sound.

A whisper—subtle but real—brushed against the silence like fingers across brittle parchment. A rustle stirred the air within the lifeless void.

The hair on Edith's nape rose. The battlefield, once echoing with cries of fury, had descended into a sinister quiet. Around her, the ruined village stood as a skeletal husk, its broken remains swallowed in creeping fog. The wind, too, had stilled. It was *too* quiet.

Her breath caught. Her instincts howled in warning.

She crouched low, muscles coiled, what remained of her wings spreading to balance her stance. Her gaze scanned the darkness with growing dread.

Then it appeared.

A shadow—not her own.

From the inky blackness of her silhouette, something began to move. It slithered forth as if tearing through the veil between realms, its form jagged and unnatural.

A **Kelxsiar.**

It crawled into being like a nightmare made flesh—elongated limbs twisting at impossible angles, abyssal eyes glowing with voidlight. Its claws, curved and glistening like obsidian, lifted into the air before slicing downward in a blur of death.

Edith reacted just in time. She twisted away, the wind of its strike screaming past her cheek. The force alone sent a shockwave through her battered form.

Teeth clenched, she retaliated. Drawing on what little strength remained, she launched into a flurry of desperate blows—fists, elbows, knees, feet. One strike. Then another. And another still. Her movements blurred with fury and pain, each impact fueled by defiance.

But the Kelxsiar didn't flinch.

Its flesh, armor-like and cold, absorbed her strikes as if they were rain against steel. Its blank eyes stared into hers with inhuman calm.

Then—it moved.

Too fast.

With one monstrous swing of its forearm—thick, gnarled, and unyielding—it struck her skull.

Crack.

A blinding flash of pain.

The world tilted.

Spiraled.

Collapsed.

Then—darkness.

II

The Great Child of Par

"In sooth, 'twas I who once bore the honor to carry forth mine own father's will—to rise as warlord of Par, as he had before me. Yet, fate did not suffer it to be so. I fear I brought shame upon his name, for I fled to realms unknown whilst he perished with crown still in hand. His rule, noble and fierce, died with him.

The choice I made—to forsake all I knew—was neither borne of cowardice nor without pain. Nay, it was a wound most grievous to mine own soul. 'Twas not the path of glory, nor the course of honor. But it was the only path wherein I might find peace.

For what is home, if not the place where the heart may rest without fear? Where one's breath may not tremble, and the soul finds its stillness? That, I say, is where mine heart hath made its dwelling."

6

Home

An echo reverberated through the chamber that housed the unconscious Edith. She floated in eerie stillness, submerged within a cylindrical tank filled with thick, gelatinous liquid that clung to her body like a second skin. A glowing respirator was affixed tightly to her face, casting soft pulses of light with every artificial breath. Wires and translucent tubes latched onto her limbs and spine, trailing outward in twitching bundles like parasitic veins, their ends disappearing into an ominous array of arcane machinery just beyond the glass. The surrounding laboratory was a grotesque fusion of desecrated sanctity and alien technology—a space that pulsed with quiet menace.

All around her, the Kelxsiar loomed. Their forms, simultaneously insectile and humanoid, shimmered in the low lighting as they stalked about the room. Cold, alien eyes bore into her suspended form, dissecting every curve of her anatomy with unfeeling precision. Their silence made their presence all the more unnerving—predators that did not speak, only watched.

In the dim, flickering glow of failing illumination, Edith's gaze settled upon something that made her chest tighten: the faded insignias scrawled along the ancient walls. Holy marks of Par— her homeland's sacred emblems—now blackened, smeared, and scoured away. They were desecrated remnants of what once was holy, erased by claw and corrosion as though the very memory of her people's divinity had been deemed unworthy to endure. This place was no mere lab—it was a sanctum twisted into something profane.

A wave of horror surged through her as realization rooted itself in her gut—she was back in Par. The Kelxsiar had dragged her, broken and unconscious, to the very hell they had made of her homeland.

Beyond the curved glass of her containment cell, the Kelxsiar moved with mounting urgency. Though sound was smothered by the tank's thick walls, Edith could see their snarls twist into expressions of alarm. Their movements became frantic, their claws flickering through the air in jagged motions. They had been experimenting on her—tampering with her body in ways she could not yet comprehend. Her limbs twitched with effort as she tried to move, but an unseen paralysis kept her frozen in place. The viscous liquid that encased her pulsed rhythmically, like a living thing exerting control, its consistency thick with sedative force. The sensation of something foreign—unnatural—moving within her veins made her stomach roil with revulsion and dread.

Then, without warning, the entire chamber shuddered.

An unnatural tremor rocked the lab to its foundations. Panic overtook the Kelxsiar. Their order collapsed into disarray as they scattered in all directions, fleeing the room like insects spooked by fire. Whatever had struck them, whatever terror had pierced their hive-mind, it was enough to send them fleeing without hesitation. In mere seconds, the chamber was vacated, and Edith was left in the deafening quiet. Her heart thundered in her chest, racing with confusion and panic. What horror had sent her captors running? What new nightmare loomed just beyond the desecrated walls of this unholy temple?

The soft hum of the surrounding machines began to fail. Lights flickered erratically, casting strobe-like shadows across the room. The arcane devices sputtered and hissed before slipping into silence. Then came the grotesque sound of shifting fluid— the gel within her tank began to thin, melting into a watery consistency before rapidly draining beneath her. Her body, no longer supported, crumpled forward, landing with a wet thud onto the cold, metallic floor.

She lay there trembling, her soaked form heaving as sensation began to return to her limbs in agonizing waves. Every nerve felt like it had been torn apart and stitched back together wrong. Her fingers twitched involuntarily, her jaw clenched to keep from crying out.

And then, the pain struck.

It started at the base of her spine and surged upward like a column of fire. Her bones screamed, muscles spasming as if something buried deep inside her had been twisted into a grotesque new shape. It was not merely pain—it was violation, the sense of her very being having been rewritten against her will. A low moan escaped her throat as she curled inward, fingers clawing at the slick floor.

Through gritted teeth, she forced herself upright, each movement a battle against weakness and torment. She inhaled sharply, dragging breath through lungs that still felt foreign. With what strength she could gather, she clenched her fists and struck the glass—once, twice, then again. Her knuckles split, her bones throbbed, but the cracks spread, thin lines of hope etched across her prison.

The fractures widened with each blow, spreading like veins of lightning across the curved glass. Then, with a final scream of defiance, the barrier gave way. The tank exploded outward in a shower of shards, the sound sharp and deafening as pieces clattered to the floor. Edith collapsed forward, gasping for air, body slick with blood and fluid.

But something was wrong.

The silence that greeted her on the other side was not one of peace—it was a silence too complete, too thick. The kind of quiet that bore teeth. The Kelxsiar were gone, yes, but not simply retreated—they had abandoned the lab entirely. She could feel it. The dread still clung to the air, heavy and waiting.

She knew she had to move. Had to escape. But she also knew, with a cold certainty pressing against her ribs, that the deeper horror—the true nightmare—awaited beyond the chamber's shattered threshold.

* * *

Across the colonial village, the air reeked of iron and death. Outside a blood-drenched medical tent, bodies lay strewn across the soil like discarded puppets, torn asunder with brutal, merciless precision. Limbs were twisted at unnatural angles, torsos split open as if clawed apart by some vengeful deity. Soldiers gathered in grim silence, their boots slick with gore, their eyes reflecting the unspeakable horror etched into the faces of their slaughtered kin. The ground beneath them was no longer earth but a canvas of ruin. The medical floor was painted in the deep crimson of spilled lives, and the scent of decay embedded itself into the very marrow of their bones, saturating their lungs with every breath they dared take.

Talbot stood at the tent's entrance, arms stiff at his sides, surveying the carnage with a hardened expression carved from years of war. Yet nothing he had witnessed—no battlefield, no siege, no massacre—could compare to this. This was no battle. This was butchery. A massacre without honor or purpose. The demon they hunted was unlike any enemy they had ever encountered.

"The beast remains at large," he muttered, the weight of the words dragging each syllable down like iron anchors. "It has taken more lives than any warlock, any heathen we have ever pursued."

One of his men, a young corporal whose hands trembled so violently his weapon clinked against his armor, gestured to the mangled remains scattered across the clearing. "What manner of unholy thing is this?" he asked, his voice tight with dread. "It does not kill for sport—it rends, it desecrates. The corpses bear no mercy."

Before Talbot could reply, a chilling scream erupted from beyond the tent, sharp and raw, cutting through the heavy fog of dread like a knife through parchment. Talbot's heart slammed against his ribs as he burst into motion, his men falling into formation with grim efficiency, rifles raised, each of them bracing for the unthinkable.

And then, he saw her.

Bethany stood amidst the corpses like a vision torn from a nightmare. A specter of death incarnate. Her presence seemed to distort the very air around her, darkening it, suffocating it. Her blackened wings, now fully unfurled, stretched wide behind her like the banner of an apocalypse. Their jagged edges shimmered with an unholy sheen. The glow of her crimson eyes bathed the trembling soldiers in an eerie, infernal light that seemed to pulse with her wrath. Blood dripped from her fingers, thick and warm, her stance unwavering. She was not a woman. She was a monument of wrath given flesh.

Talbot swallowed the lump of fear rising in his throat, clenching his jaw. He forced steel into his voice, though his fingers itched with the tremble of dread. "We have no need of words, fiend. You are condemned to hell."

Bethany tilted her head slowly, like a predator toying with prey. Her lips curled into something between a smirk and a snarl. "Hell?" she mused, her voice a venomous whisper that slithered through the cold air. "Thou dost not ken what hell is."

Her words slithered into their ears like serpents, cold and paralyzing. The temperature seemed to drop as an unseen pressure crushed the atmosphere.

Talbot stiffened, shaking off the chill that wormed down his spine. He raised his rifle. "Fire," he commanded.

The crack of gunfire exploded into the night. Smoke and fire roared from the barrels, and lead screamed through the air toward her.

And in less than a breath, she was gone.

In a blur of motion beyond mortal comprehension, Bethany vanished. Her form reappeared behind one soldier, then beside another, darting like a shadow made of blades. Panic erupted. Bullets sliced through nothing but smoke and specter. The soldiers fired in desperation, their lines collapsing into disarray as they turned to follow her impossible movement. A scream rang out as one soldier's throat was torn open, his blood spraying in a graceful arc that painted the darkness red. Another was lifted into the air with terrifying ease, his body writhing in agony before being hurled into his comrades like a shattered doll, bones snapping audibly upon impact.

Bethany's rage had awakened something monstrous.

Something ancient. Something beyond any horror they had faced in war or myth.

And she would not stop.

Not until they all suffered as she had.

* * *

The red night skies of Par burned with an unnatural brilliance. Jagged streaks of light—blinding, searing, violent—sliced through the darkness like divine spears cast by vengeful gods. The air was thick with the acrid stench of charred flesh, of metal warped and melting beneath the relentless bombardment. Edith stumbled forward, her breath ragged, her body still weak from the Kelxsiar's torturous grasp. This… this was not the home she remembered.

This was something else entirely.

The invaders struck with terrifying precision, beams of energy descending like the wrath of a vengeful deity, carving through the alien landscape with unrelenting fury. The Kelxsiar scrambled,

131

shrieking in their guttural, nightmarish tongues, their monstrous forms twisting and writhing in disarray. They did not know where the attack was coming from. They were the apex predators of this realm, yet here they stood—hunted, slaughtered like vermin in their own den.

A brilliant light detonated the ground near Edith, the sheer force of the blast hurling her backward. She landed hard, the impact rattling her bones, pain singing through her body. Smoke and dust choked the air. Her vision blurred, but as it cleared, a shadow emerged from the blinding radiance before her.

It was no Kelxsiar.

The being stood tall, its form an eerie construct of bioluminescent flesh, veins of golden energy pulsating beneath its semi-translucent skin. The patterns shifted like a living constellation, moving with an intelligence beyond comprehension. The creature's eyes, hollow yet filled with sentient light, bore into her with an intensity that sent a shudder down her spine.

"You are not Kelxsiar," the being said. Its voice did not come from its mouth but echoed directly in her mind, an overwhelming presence that vibrated through her skull. "Come with me. This world is set to die."

Edith flinched at the words, struggling to push

herself up. Her muscles screamed in protest, but she forced herself to her knees, staring up at the luminous entity. Its outstretched appendage—long, sinewy, and pulsing with golden filaments of light—waited.

"What are you?" she rasped, her throat raw from dust and exhaustion.

"No time for questions. If you wish to live, take my hand."

A cold, insidious fear curled in her gut. She had no reason to trust this being, no assurance that it was any less of a threat than the Kelxsiar. And yet… something in its voice—its presence—felt different. Unlike the Kelxsiar's hunger and cruelty, this creature radiated purpose.

And the world around them was dying.

Her hand trembled as she reached forward, her fingers brushing against the being's outstretched limb. The moment they touched, a deafening *crack* split the air. A pulse of raw energy erupted around them, faster and louder than lightning, swallowing the battlefield in a surge of blinding white.

Then, nothing.

Silence.

Edith gasped as she opened her eyes. White light engulfed her, endless, suffocating, vast. She could see nothing beyond the blinding radiance, hear nothing except the erratic pound of her own heartbeat. Then, as swiftly as it had come, the suffocating light faded, and her senses sharpened.

A cold, metallic pressure encased her head, and the sudden weight made her panic. She reached up, her hands colliding with something smooth, something solid. A helmet. Before she could react, a voice—deep, resonant—filled her mind once more.

"We mean you no harm."

Her breathing slowed, her fingers loosening against the strange headpiece. The light dimmed just enough for her to make out the figure before her—another of the glowing beings, its form outlined with radiant energy.

"What are you?" she asked again, this time more demanding.

"Halphobs," the being answered. "Th-Gil Realm is our origin."

Edith's mind reeled. Th-Gil? A name she had only heard whispered in the halls of her father's war councils.

"Why are you on Par?" she pressed.

The Halphob's glow pulsed, as if considering its answer. "Your people illegally imprisoned our soldiers. We are here to bring them home."

Edith's chest tightened. "My people are dead."

"And yet my kind dims within your world."

She hesitated, her mind racing, unraveling the

implications. "Why did my father wage war against you?"

The being's form brightened, its luminescence intensifying. "Your father is the warlord?" It was not a question. It was a revelation.

"He was," Edith said, her voice low, heavy with the weight of a past she wished to bury. "I disowned his memory the moment I realized he had forsaken my only kin."

Silence stretched between them. The Halphob turned away, gazing through a transparent panel—Edith realized now that she was aboard a vessel, its sleek interior humming with quiet, alien energy. Below them, the surface of Par was ablaze, the Kelxsiar strongholds falling one after another under the relentless assault of the Halphob invasion.

The being exhaled a sound that was neither a sigh nor a breath. "Your father murdered trillions, most not in the theater of war. It was theft of resources. Unmatched greed."

Edith swallowed, her throat thick with something she could not name. "Why did he imprison your kind?"

The Halphob's glow darkened, shifting toward a deep amber. "Because we opposed his crimes. We resisted. We are not a people of war, but we would not stand idly by. Your kind knows only destruction, terror."

Edith clenched her fists. "I am not my father. I only wish to bring peace." Her voice trembled, but not with fear. With conviction. "My people—what's left of them—are scattered. Hunted. If I can save them, I will."

The Halphob leader observed her, its body flickering with unreadable emotion.

"We have always wanted peace," it said at last. "But we want our people freed."

Edith stepped forward, her golden eyes gleaming. "Give me your mercy, and I will fight with you to bring liberty to your realmers. The Kelxsiar will not be allowed to continue my father's crimes."

The being regarded her for a long moment before nodding once.

"You have my word," Edith said, her voice unyielding.

The Halphob's glow intensified. "And we shall hold you to it."

Below them, Par burned.

And war, once again, began.

Edith sat in the cold, hollow embrace of the machine, her body tethered to it by a network of luminous wires. They pulsed with energy, their intricate veins of light threading into the helmet affixed to her skull. It was neither pain nor comfort—only a vast emptiness that stretched beyond the confines of sensation. Her thoughts felt suspended, floating somewhere between consciousness and oblivion.

All around her, the world ceased to exist.

She was no longer on the Halphob ship. No longer in Par. No longer *anywhere*.

Instead, she sat within an *infinite void of white*, a blinding eternity of nothingness. It swallowed everything, devoured the very concept of form and space, leaving only herself—adrift in a sea of infinite possibility. Was this death? Or something far worse?

A voice, deep and omnipotent, slithered into her mind, bypassing all barriers of language or restraint.

"It seems they merely ran tests on you. Nothing more."

The words were not spoken in sound but *imprinted* upon her very being, resonating like an ancient pulse that carried the weight of time itself.

Commander Tilk.

His voice was vast, layered, as if every syllable was woven from the accumulated wisdom of a thousand civilizations. To hear him speak was to feel a consciousness pressing against her own, as though his very words were peeling back the layers of her mind, analyzing every thought before it was even formed.

Edith swallowed, her own voice feeling pitifully *small* in comparison. "I wish I knew *what* they were testing for."

As soon as she spoke, the void trembled. Reality shifted. The unbearable whiteness peeled away like fragile silk, unraveling until the world around her *shuddered* back into existence.

She was no longer floating. No longer lost in nothingness.

She was *back*—seated within the Halphob vessel, wires still clinging to her flesh, the metal beneath her humming with unseen energy. The glow of the ship's interior was almost *painfully* sharp now, a contrast to the soulless void she had just left.

Commander Tilk stood before her, his luminous form flickering in an eerie rhythm. His bio luminescent veins pulsed like a nebula constricting in deep space, shifting from their usual golden brilliance into a deeper, more ominous red.

"It does not matter," he said at last, his tone unreadable. *"Their species is to be cleansed."*

Edith felt something tighten in her gut.

She had seen slaughter before. She had been raised in war. But there was something *cold* about the way he said it—no anger, no hatred. Just an immutable fact. Like the movement of celestial bodies or the passage of time.

"This is genocide," Edith whispered, her words

barely audible.

Tilk's glow dimmed further, his form vibrating with something she could *not* comprehend.

"Your grasp of the situation is... disappointingly simplistic." His voice was smooth, calculated—like an artist patiently explaining the mechanics of their masterpiece to a child who could never hope to understand.

"For millennia, we have stood as guardians of equilibrium, architects of a peace we never sought to impose— but merely hoped to maintain. And what has been our reward? Betrayal. Bloodshed. We have witnessed countless lesser creatures twist our benevolence into weakness, abuse our forbearance as an invitation to strike first. So tell me, Edith of Par... should we simply wait to be slaughtered next? Shall we extend mercy to those who have no concept of it?"

Edith's fingers twitched.

"I didn't say it was *wrong*."

"Your hesitation implies it."

The glow of Tilk's body flickered again— darkening, deepening. The once golden veins of light coursing through him had now bled into a deep, *angry* crimson. It was a warning, as clear as the edge of a blade pressed against a throat.

Edith's heart pounded. She forced herself to remain still, to keep her breath even.

"I need a favor," she said finally, her voice careful.

"Once we rescue your people."

The air around Tilk *shifted,* as if the very space within the ship bent in accordance with his mood.

"A *favor?*" he repeated, the word dripping with amusement.

Edith inhaled sharply. "There is a realm. A place where the last of my kind resides. My only kin. She and I… had *disagreements.* But I need to return."

Tilk remained motionless, the steady pulse of his form the only indication that he was still present.

"*The Par engineered the Voidspire Engines,*" he said at last, each syllable measured, dissected. "*Your kind was once powerful enough to bend the very fabric of existence, to carve paths between realms like a sculptor shaping stone. And yet now you stand before me— powerless, diminished. A remnant of a ruined dynasty.*"

"The Kelxsiar destroyed them," Edith admitted, her voice tight. "They did *not* want our kind to return. They fear the idea that distant survivors may rise and reclaim what was lost."

Tilk was silent for a long moment.

"*Your safety is not assured.*"

Edith's stomach twisted.

"*Your survival is irrelevant.*"

She clenched her fists.

"*But we shall consider your request.*"

The words did not bring comfort. They were not *meant* to.

Tilk's gaze bore into her, his eyes hollow, unreadable.

"Fail us... and you will be abandoned. You will be left to rot in this broken world, as your kind has always done. If you falter in this task, Edith of Par, know that our mercy will not extend to you."

The air in the room felt suffocating, thick with unspoken threats.

Edith forced herself to meet his gaze.

"I have everything to lose," she said, her voice unwavering. "I will *not* fail."

Tilk studied her for a long, agonizing moment. Then, slowly, his form brightened again, shifting back to a golden hue.

"See that you do not."

Outside the ship, the skies of Par continued to burn. And below, amidst the carnage, the last war of the Par Realmers had only just begun.

* * *

The air was thick with the metallic tang of blood, though the battle had not yet begun. The night held its breath, the moon glaring down like the eye of a silent, indifferent god. Talbot knelt behind the crumbling wall of an abandoned house, his hands ghosting over his rifle. His fingers trembled—perhaps from the cold, perhaps from the knowledge that what they were hunting was no longer human.

Behind him, his men fanned out in practiced formation, their footsteps muffled against the earth, their figures barely discernible in the darkness. They had stalked death before, but never like this. Never *her*.

For days, they had been pursuing a demon. A nightmare with wings darker than the void, with eyes like burning coals buried deep within a crimson mask of rage. They had found the mutilated remains of their comrades torn apart, bodies defiled beyond recognition, the entrails left to steam in the cold air as if their torment had been an offering.

And now, Talbot and his remaining men—fifteen soldiers, each carrying the weight of their own silent dread—approached the last known location of the monster.

The village stood abandoned, its streets eerie and desolate, the houses hunched over like mourning specters. The air reeked of decay, the scent of death embedded deep within the earth itself. The silence was unnatural.

A low whistle cut through the night. A signal.

One of Talbot's men pointed ahead, his trembling fingers betraying his discipline.

There she stood.

At the very edge of the village, framed by the skeletal trees of the forest beyond, Bethany waited.

She did not move. Did not flinch.

Her arms were outstretched at her sides, as if in communion with some unseen force, her body still as stone. The wind lifted her tattered dress, the hem soaked in the blood of those she had already slaughtered.

She knew they were coming. She *felt* them. Their fear was a palpable thing, an electric pulse that set her teeth on edge. It was intoxicating.

Talbot's heart pounded against his ribs. He raised his hand sharply, then dropped it.

Attack.

The soldiers surged forward, boots pounding the dirt, their breaths ragged with adrenaline.

Bethany moved.

A sickening, bestial roar tore through the air as she *spun* with unnatural speed, her black wings unfurling like the appendages of some ancient god of ruin. The inky aura that bled from her body twisted and writhed as though it possessed a hunger of its own.

Then she *leapt*—

A streak of darkness against the moon, a flash of crimson eyes, and then—

Screams.

Talbot barely registered the first man being

ripped from the ground, his body jerked violently into the air. Bethany's wings snatched him with the precision of a hunter's snare, then *tore him apart* in mid-flight. The air exploded with blood, a mist of gore spraying down upon the soldiers as what remained of their comrade was flung into the trees.

Chaos.

Gunfire erupted, desperate and blind.

She was among them before they could react.

Her claws *sang* through flesh, slicing effortlessly through muscle and bone. She moved like liquid shadow, a predator unhindered by mortal limitations. Her fingers sank into a soldier's chest, piercing skin and ribs alike, her grip finding his trembling heart. He didn't even have time to scream before she *ripped it free*, the warmth of his final breath still lingering on his lips as he collapsed lifelessly at her feet.

Another swung at her, his bayonet catching the moonlight, but Bethany caught his wrist in an iron grip. With a guttural snarl, she *tore* his arm clean from his body. The soldier's shriek of agony barely lasted a second before she swung the severed limb like a cudgel, smashing another soldier's face into a pulpy ruin.

The ground became slick with blood.

Six men encircled her, their weapons raised in shaking hands.

Bethany smiled, baring jagged teeth that gleamed wet with gore.

They rushed her at once.

She was a whirlwind of death, her body weaving between their strikes with a grace that mocked their frantic desperation. A bayonet thrust—*sidestep*. A musket fire—*duck, lunge, disembowel*. A desperate swing of a blade—*catch, twist, snap*.

One soldier stumbled back, clutching his stomach, his intestines unraveling like rope from the gaping wound Bethany had carved into him.

Another screamed as she caught him mid-strike, her claws burying into his throat. She lifted him effortlessly, his feet kicking uselessly against the air before she *bit down*—

Her jaw unhinged, stretching impossibly wide, her fangs sinking deep into the soft flesh of his neck. The soldier gurgled, his body convulsing as she *tore his head clean from his shoulders*.

She spat the skull aside, tossing the decapitated corpse like a ragdoll into the crumbling remains of a house. The force of the impact shattered the building's foundation, causing it to *collapse in on itself*.

Talbot barely had time to react.

He moved, *instinct* guiding him, and swung his rifle like a club.

The stock of the weapon *slammed* into the back

of Bethany's head.

It should have sent her reeling. Should have *stunned* her.

It didn't.

Bethany turned slowly, her eyes blazing brighter, her body shuddering as something within her *shifted*.

Talbot stumbled back.

Her form was changing—her horns lengthening, her claws extending further into needle-sharp talons. Her crimson skin pulsed with glowing fissures of molten black, like fire cracking through charred wood.

She looked like something *born* from the deepest pits of the abyss.

And she was smiling.

Before Talbot could raise his weapon, Bethany *lunged*, her clawed hand wrapping around his throat.

His breath hitched, pain searing through his body as her grip *tightened*, the heat of her skin scalding his flesh. He clawed at her wrist, but it was *impossible*—she was too strong. His vision blurred, his pulse thundered, his lungs burned for air.

A gunshot rang out.

Bethany flinched, a bullet *slamming* into the side of her skull.

Her grip faltered.

Talbot collapsed to the ground, gasping for air.

One of his remaining men fired again, and Bethany snarled, turning toward him with *inhuman fury*.

She moved in a blur, catching the soldier mid-reload, lifting him off his feet. With one brutal motion, she *ripped* his spine from his body, tossing the lifeless husk aside like discarded meat.

Talbot barely had time to react before Bethany's wing *smashed* into his chest.

The force of it sent him flying *through* the trees, his body breaking branches as he hurtled through the air.

Then—*darkness*.

He crashed hard against the forest floor, his body broken, breathless.

The world tilted, his vision blurred, the stars above warping into streaks of light.

And then—*nothing.*

The void took him.

Bethany stood amidst the carnage, the battlefield *hers* now.

She had become what they feared.

And she *wasn't done yet.*

7

The Will to Fight

The Kelxsiar were the eternal wardens of suffering, monstrous sentinels born from a pitiless void. Their bodies were twisted, grotesque amalgamations of sinew and obsidian flesh, and their minds were riddled with bloodlust and primitive cunning. For cycles uncounted, they had stood watch over the Dungeons of Par—a festering wound carved deep beneath the decayed bones of a kingdom long since drowned in war.

The air was thick with the reek of rot and despair. Screams no longer echoed here; those who still lived had long since abandoned the energy to cry out. Blood, blackened by time, marred the walls like crude art, and the floor was layered with the remnants of those who had once dared to resist. It was a realm of the condemned—a place where light was a foreign concept.

Until now.

The Halphobs stood within their cells, silent and motionless, their glowing forms barely illuminating the filth-ridden chambers. Their bodies, woven from pulsating luminescence and shifting organic circuitry, were paradoxes—beings of peace imprisoned in a world ruled by carnage. Unlike the other captives, they did not tremble. They did not despair. They simply watched.

A Kelxsiar warden lumbered forward, its jagged teeth clacking as it dragged a rusted blade across the cell bars. The sound shrieked through the corridors like a chorus of tortured souls. Its gnarled lips curled back in a sneer, and its eyes glinted with malice.

"You's no fight. You's weak. Glow-things surrender. Tell weak ones outside… go home!"

One of the Halphobs turned its head in a slow, fluid movement, as though each motion carried the weight of incomprehensible intelligence. Its radiant form flickered—like a star contemplating whether to collapse or expand. When it spoke, it did not use words. It invaded the Kelxsiar's mind. The voice was not spoken, nor whispered, but imposed—a tidal wave of logic that burned like white-hot steel.

"Your war is lost."

The Kelxsiar snarled and recoiled as if struck. Its

clawed fingers flexed in agitation, scraping against the metal bars.

"Kelxsiar never lose! Never bow!"

"Your defiance is statistical folly," the Halphob replied. Its glowing eyes intensified, boring into the Kelxsiar's consciousness like an inescapable truth. *"Your forces dwindle. Your stronghold fractures. You have no reinforcements. Your refusal to submit does not change reality."*

The Kelxsiar's breath heaved in rage, but something primal inside its ancient mind began to shudder. A thought it had never dared to entertain whispered like a ghost in the back of its skull:

What if we are truly dying?

Then the sky itself collapsed.

A roaring explosion of blinding golden light tore through the prison ceiling, raining shards of molten stone down upon the hellish corridors. The dungeon trembled—its ancient foundations splintering beneath the celestial wrath that had been unleashed.

And from the sky, descending like a divine blade sent to carve judgment into stone, came Edith.

Her wings unfurled—massive and luminous— their brilliant white plumage stark against the abyssal darkness of the prison. She landed amid the chaos, her armored boots crunching against rubble. Her golden gaze burned with righteous fury. The air around her hummed with raw power, the weight of a bloodline steeped in war and regret pressed into her every breath.

She raised her hand toward the Kelxsiar ranks. Her voice rang out—a command, unshakable and absolute—shattering the silence like a war cry carved into the marrow of the universe itself.

"Release the prisoners."

The Kelxsiar warriors, despite their monstrous resilience, faltered. They could feel the power radiating from her, a force so intense it bent the very reality around her. Their talons flexed. Their grotesque forms tensed.

And then they roared.

"PAR IS DEAD!"

Edith tilted her head, unmoved.

"I am alive."

The moment the words left her lips, the heavens answered.

A pillar of divine energy detonated from above— a beam of celestial vengeance lancing through the Kelxsiar ranks. The searing force scorched through flesh and bone, reducing the wardens to writhing, smoldering husks. Their shrieks filled the dungeon, a symphony of agony swallowed by blinding, unrelenting light.

From the shadows, more Kelxsiar surged forward—flickering with rage-induced speed, their bodies twisting through the air, claws outstretched.

Lightning split the darkness.

The Halphobs materialized in a crackling storm of energy, their forms woven from plasma and raw intelligence. They moved with impossible precision, each gesture calculated down to the microsecond. Their light-forged weapons carved through the Kelxsiar like scalpels slicing through diseased flesh.

The battle became a slaughter.

Edith danced through the carnage. Her strikes crushed bone and shattered limbs. Her blade painted the walls with tar-black Kelxsiar blood. Her wings moved like a tempest, tearing through the air and hammering her enemies into ruin.

One Kelxsiar lunged—she spun, slammed her knee into its ribs, then drove her blade through its gaping maw. The creature gurgled as golden fire consumed it from the inside out. Another grappled her, claws digging deep into her shoulder—she wrenched free, her wing slicing through its arm. It reeled back, howling, before she caved in its skull with a single, brutal punch.

"Edith!"

A Halphob lieutenant called through the chaos, its voice crisp despite the devastation.

She turned, her face streaked with blood and war light.

"These prisoners will not survive if they stay here. Get them to the temple."

Her eyes flickered with hesitation.

"I cannot activate a Voidspire Engine. It has been too long."

"Then you must remember."

She stiffened. The legacy of her bloodline— the architects of war, the destroyers of worlds— loomed behind her like a shadow. She gritted her teeth, then nodded.

Turning toward the cells, she raised her hand. With a sweeping gesture, the doors melted away. The rusted metal dripped like wax, and the restraints that had bound the condemned for generations fell to the floor with a finality that silenced the very air.

The prisoners stepped forward—some hesitant, others collapsing to their knees in disbelief.

Outside, beneath the bleeding-red sky of Par, they gazed upon their shattered world one last time.

Edith turned to face them. Her voice was calm, unwavering.

"The journey is long, but it is the only path forward. Stay with me, and I will take you to something better."

A murmur rippled through the crowd—fear, uncertainty, disbelief.

Then a man stepped forward, his body scarred, his eyes burning with old rage.

"Why should we trust you?" he asked, his voice hoarse but defiant. "Your father's blood still runs in your veins. It was he who doomed us."

Edith held his gaze, unwavering.

"And it is my will that undoes him."

Silence followed.

Then, the man lowered his head.

One by one, the prisoners followed her into the wasteland.

Edith led them forward, her wings casting long, defiant shadows across the ruins of a world that had forsaken them all.

A wretched figure staggered behind Edith, its breath rattling in its chest like something broken and wet. Every step it took sounded labored, dragging against the cracked and splintered ground of the dying realm. The rest of the prisoners followed in uneasy silence, their gaunt faces flickering in and out of the dim glow cast by the sky's bleeding red horizon.

Edith didn't stop. She kept moving, her boots kicking up dust and bone fragments as she led them through Par's decaying landscape. She could still feel the heat of war on her skin—the echoes of slaughter vibrating through the air like a dying heartbeat. They didn't have much time.

"I know where you're taking us," the voice rasped from behind her.

Edith turned slightly, catching a glimpse of the speaker. He was an eerie, misshapen thing—his body etched with glowing ritualistic lines, his back twisted by unnatural protrusions that twitched beneath his skin, as though something inside him were trying to break free.

"Knowing is one thing," Edith said, her tone sharp. "Trusting me will keep you alive."

A thin, humorless chuckle rattled from his throat. "Alive? That's what you think this is?" He gestured toward the barren wasteland around them, where skeletal trees stretched like twisted fingers toward the crimson sky. "This is a graveyard. You're just guiding us to a different tomb."

Edith ignored him. Her wings twitched with impatience. She didn't need his cynicism. She needed to get them to the Firmament Temple before the world collapsed beneath them.

"Yes… lead us to the shrine of your cursed bloodline," the figure continued, his voice dripping with something venomous. "The place where your people prayed to their false gods before they slaughtered mine."

Edith clenched her jaw. "No one's forcing you to follow. You're free to stay in the cursed world."

The creature's blackened lips curled into something between a sneer and a grimace. "Cursed? You're the one that's cursed. You and your hideous kin. Oh, you don't even know, do you?" He let out a wheezing laugh, sharp and rusted at the edges. "Your father must have kept so many secrets."

That made her stop.

Edith turned fully to face him now, motioning for the others to keep going. She stared at him, her golden eyes sharp and unyielding. "What the hell are you talking about?"

The creature took a slow, deliberate step toward her. The air between them thickened, charged with something dark—something ancient and cold.

"You really don't know?" He exhaled and shook his head. "How poetic."

"Talk," Edith demanded, her voice laced with ice.

The figure tilted his head, studying her. "We were called the Nerl. Before your father came."

Edith's breath hitched slightly. She had heard that name before—once, maybe twice—buried in whispers, spoken only by those who barely dared to remember.

"We were a peaceful people," the Nerl continued, his voice low and bitter. "We didn't crave war. We didn't need it. And yet your father brought it to us. He invaded our realm, took what he wanted—our magic, our knowledge—and when we resisted, he made sure we burned for it."

Edith swallowed hard, trying to suppress the growing sickness in her gut.

"You survived," she said, though it felt more like a question than a statement.

The Nerl's gaze darkened. "If you call this surviving." He flexed his hands, and the glow from his markings pulsed weakly. "Without the life-force of my realm, my kind withered. Some of us decayed. Others… changed."

Edith's eyes drifted to the jagged protrusions lining his back. "You were trapped here."

"For centuries," the Nerl whispered. "Starving. Waiting."

Edith exhaled slowly through her nose, her mind racing. "What do you want from me?"

The Nerl's eyes gleamed in the dim light. "To make things right."

"I can't bring back the dead," she said, her voice more grounded than she felt.

"No," the Nerl admitted. "But you can at least acknowledge what was done." He stepped closer, his voice dropping lower, more intimate. "Tell me… did your father ever speak of the curse?"

Edith's pulse stilled.

"What curse?" she asked slowly.

The Nerl's expression twisted into something unreadable, something ancient and sorrowful.

"He never told you?" A quiet, broken laugh slipped past his lips. "Of course he didn't. He feared it. He feared her."

Her blood ran cold.

The Nerl leaned in, his voice a whisper of old pain. "Skin red as a bleeding sun. Horns, twisted like the roots of corruption. Eyes black as the void your people created."

Edith's breath hitched.

No…

Kore.

The word struck her like a hammer to the chest. The grotesque features Kore had been born with—the ones their father had deemed monstrous, unworthy of a place in his kingdom. He had exiled her, hated her, rejected her. And for what? Because she was different? Because she had been born with features no other Par Realmer possessed?

Or had it been something else?

Something darker?

Edith's hands curled into fists as realization gripped her like ice. "Are you saying she was cursed?"

The Nerl's black eyes bore into hers, hollow and heavy with truth.

"Not just cursed," he murmured.

His lips parted into something that might have once been a grin—crooked, tired, and full of rot.

"She was designed to be damned."

* * *

Talbot woke with a shuddering gasp, the very breath in his lungs feeling stolen. His fingers clutched at the rough wool beneath him, his senses drowned in the mingled stench of sweat, blood, and death. The air was thick with it, the sickly-sweet rot of the dying clinging to the canvas walls like a ghost.

A candle flickered, casting long shadows over the rows of cots. Some bore men writhing in fevered agony, their bodies ravaged by wounds ill-tended. Others lay still, their forms draped in linen, the mark of the ferryman's due.

Talbot's chest heaved as he pushed himself upright, his limbs heavy with pain. This was no battlefield, no place for swords to clash nor drums to sound. This was a den of the forsaken.

"Ho! Who goes there?" His voice rasped, breaking the eerie silence. He turned his head sharply. "Who sees to this place?"

No answer.

A chill crept over him, slow and insidious. His breath quickened.

"I say again! Does no man attend his post?"

A rustling at the tent's entrance. A shape in the

candlelight.

"Talbot!"

Cornish. His bearing was feebler than before, his once-proud stance undone by injury. His right arm was bound tight, a dark stain creeping through the bandage, and his left hand trembled at his side.

Talbot fixed him with a steely glare. "Cornish, what madness is this? Why have I been pulled from the field? Speak plainly!"

Cornish's throat bobbed, his face wan as though he had swallowed some bitter draught. "There was no field, Talbot. Not as thou think'st it."

Talbot's brows furrowed. "Do not trifle with me. I recall the battle. The steel in my grip, the cries of our men, the charge against the beast—"

"Aye, and what came of it?" Cornish cut him off, voice trembling. "Dost thou think we gave fair fight? We were not soldiers upon that ground—we were lambs led to slaughter! No war was waged this night, but a reckoning!"

Talbot's fists clenched. "Damn thy riddles, Cornish! How many yet stand?"

Cornish's lips parted, yet for a moment, no words came. His gaze dropped, as though he feared to meet Talbot's eyes.

"None."

Talbot felt the breath leave him. "None?"

Cornish shook his head, his voice but a whisper.

"Our company is gone, Talbot. There remains none to tell the tale but we."

Talbot's pulse thundered in his ears. "And the villages?" he demanded, his tone sharp, unyielding.

Cornish exhaled through his nose, his fingers flexing, as though grasping for something unseen. "None know for certain. Mayhap hundreds lay dead. Mayhap thousands." His voice caught. "Mayhap more."

A shadow passed over Talbot's face, though his stance held firm. He ground his teeth. "Then this cannot stand. If what thou speak'st be true, we must send word. One man must ride west to the garrisons. We needs must have reinforcements, muskets, cannon—"

Cornish let out a low, humorless laugh. "Thou dost not understand, dost thou? Reinforcements? Steel? Shot? What think'st thou these will do?" His voice cracked, his eyes dark with something between sorrow and terror. "I saw it, Talbot. As didst thou. Our blades touched it, yet harmed it not. The beast laughed at our pikes and pistols! Laughed! As though we were gnats swatted from its path!"

"Enough!" Talbot barked, though his breath came heavier now. He willed himself not to remember, not to see it again—the thing that had risen from the darkness, the thing that had moved like no creature of God's design.

Cornish's shoulders slumped. "Thou dost know it, same as I. There is naught to be done but flee."

"Nay," Talbot said, his voice iron. He set his jaw, his fingers curling into fists. "There is always something to be done."

Cornish stared at him, a flicker of disbelief in his weary eyes. "Talbot—"

Talbot straightened, every aching muscle rebelling against him, yet he did not yield. "I saw the beast with mine own eyes, and like any creature, it may yet fall. There is no thing upon this earth without weakness. It bled, did it not?"

Cornish hesitated, his breath shallow. "...Aye. I did see it bleed."

"Then it may die," Talbot said darkly.

Cornish exhaled through his nose, shaking his head. "Thou art a fool."

"Then I shall die a fool."

Talbot reached for the blade at his side, though his fingers trembled as they wrapped around the hilt.

Cornish watched him for a long moment. Then, at last, he spoke.

"Then thou art already dead."

The candle wavered, its light shrinking as if the very air conspired to snuff it out.

And outside, beyond the frail walls of the tent,

something stirred.

Something listening.

Something waiting.

***

The weight of revelation bore down on Edith like an iron shackle, an inescapable truth tightening around her mind with every step. Her sister—her own blood—was yet another casualty in the endless cycle of suffering their father had wrought. His hatred ran so deep, so absolute, that not even the ties of flesh and kinship had been enough to shield Kore from his wrath. The realization clung to Edith's spine like frost, numbing and relentless.

She pressed forward, leading the exodus through the desolate landscape. Her gaze remained fixed on the ruin that loomed ahead—the skeletal remains of the once-magnificent Firmament Temple. It stood broken and silent, crumbling stone and fractured spires stretching desperately toward the ashen sky like the hands of the damned. The air was dry, sour with ash and memory. Once, warriors had knelt here before battle, pledging their blades to gods whose names were now lost to time. Now, the temple lay abandoned, a mausoleum for faith, its prayers drowned beneath centuries of dust and blood.

"It's here," Edith murmured, her voice hushed and frayed, a fragile strand of hope woven into exhaustion.

Beside her, the Nerl moved with guarded tension. His odd features were tight, jaw clenched, slitted eyes flicking uneasily between her and the temple's husk. "And if it's not?" he asked, his tone sharp, laced with a rising edge of restrained panic.

Edith hesitated. She wanted to answer with confidence, to offer the illusion of control. But there was none to give. No plan, no strategy—just blind hope in a realm that had long since begun to rot from the inside out. The truth hung between them like a drawn blade.

"Then I guess we stay here," she said finally, her words brittle, edged in the cold weight of resignation.

The moment her words left her lips, the ground trembled.

At first, it was subtle—a whisper beneath their boots, the faint groan of a sleeping giant. Then the tremor deepened, shaking the earth in heavy, bone-jarring pulses. Dust surged from the ruins. Cracks split across stone and soil. The sky itself seemed to flinch.

These weren't earthquakes.

They were footsteps.

Something massive was drawing near, each step a thunderclap that echoed across the dead world. The air shifted, thickening like tar, weighted with dread. A sound followed—low, guttural, vile. It tore through the silence like claws on bone, vibrating through marrow and memory.

A roar.

Deep and terrible. Ancient and alive.

Edith's blood turned to ice. She had heard that sound before—in dreams that bled into waking, in nightmares passed down like scars.

A Hunter.

The beast's presence rolled across them like a stormfront. The survivors stilled, their breaths caught in throats too afraid to tremble. The very wind seemed to halt in reverence—or fear.

"It's their beast," the Nerl hissed beside her, his voice tight and cracking. His hands curled into trembling fists. "They sent it to finish what they started."

"Stand your ground," Edith commanded, pivoting to face the haggard assembly behind her—those broken wretches who had entrusted their fate to her dwindling strength. "If we fight, we live!"

"No!" the Nerl cried, the word a raw explosion of panic. He staggered back, shaking violently, his composure fracturing like glass. "We trusted you! And you led us into a slaughterhouse!"

"Calm yourself!" Edith snapped, stepping forward.

But it was too late. Madness had taken root in him.

"You're not taking me!" he screamed, his voice unraveling into hysteria. "You and your kind can rot together—in the bowels of this forsaken hell!"

He bolted, fleeing into the wastes like a shadow torn loose from the ground. His limbs pumped with frantic energy, eyes wild, body moving on terror alone.

The roar came again—closer this time. And then the world seemed to explode.

From the haze emerged the beast, a wall of hunger and muscle, its form impossible to fully comprehend. Its skin shimmered with the colors of rot and dusk. Glowing eyes seared through the darkness, locking instantly onto the Nerl.

Then it struck.

The creature closed the distance in an instant, faster than anything that size should be. Its jaws clamped down with a sickening crunch, severing the Nerl's scream mid-breath. Bones snapped like brittle wood. Flesh tore in wet, awful shreds. The Nerl's body was wrenched in two with horrific ease, a spray of blood arcing high before falling in hot, steaming ribbons upon the desecrated ground.

Edith flinched, her breath caught in her throat.

The Hunter raised its head, bits of sinew hanging from its maw, the remains of its kill clutched in claws that could tear through steel.

And then—its gaze shifted.

Those blazing orbs of otherworldly fire turned to Edith and the remaining survivors.

The hunt was not over.

It had only just begun.

* * *

The farmhouse groaned beneath the weight of fear.

Its weathered beams creaked like brittle bones, each sound echoing through the silence as if the very walls were bracing for what came next. Shadows stretched long across the dirt-caked floor, their edges sharp and clawed like talons seeking flesh. In every corner, peasants huddled in desperate prayer—mothers clutching children, elders whispering old rites under their breath, men pressing crude tools to their chests like talismans.

A woman near the center of the room gripped her daughter to her breast, her trembling hands pressing the girl's face tightly against her tattered bodice in a futile attempt to muffle her sobs. The child whimpered softly, her voice too young to understand terror but old enough to feel it in her bones. The air was thick with the scent of sweat and stale hay—but beneath it lingered something darker. A sour rot. The copper tang of blood yet to be spilled, clinging to the back of the throat like a curse already cast.

Outside, the night shuddered with the presence of something unholy.

A low growl slithered through the chill air, coiling between the cracks in the timber, setting nails to quivering and rattling the dry thatch of the roof. It was not the growl of a beast, nor of any mortal predator. It was something deeper—more primal. A sound that carried with it the weight of forgotten nightmares and long-buried sins.

Kore was near.

She and the darkness were bound together, not merely by the absence of light but by a covenant far more insidious—an ancient accord between monster and abyss. The void was her cradle, her lover, her confessional. And in its suffocating embrace, she had long since been absolved of guilt, pity, or restraint.

A single child's sob cracked the silence like a shard of glass shattering against stone.

The mother's hand clamped tighter over her daughter's mouth, but it was already too late. Kore had caught their scent—the reek of despair and trembling hope, of unworthy souls perfuming the air like spiced meat offered to a ravenous god.

The barn doors exploded inward.

A cacophony of shrieking iron and splintering wood rent through the night as the massive double doors tore from their hinges. They flew inward like broken wings, flung by a force beyond comprehension. Peasants screamed and scattered, arms flailing as they were hurled across the room by the blast of air and debris. Dust billowed, choking lungs and blinding eyes, and in that swirling haze of dread and ash, she appeared.

Kore.

A twisted effigy of what had once been divine, now deformed by wrath and corrupted purpose.

Her wings jutted from her back like the skeletal remains of a fallen angel, each malformed feather serrated, dripping with the ichor of sins long consumed. Claws, elongated and gnarled, clicked together as she flexed them in anticipation—each talon a promise of agony. From her brow, two massive horns curved forward like the war banners of Hell itself, their ridged edges slick with blood both ancient and new. Firelight danced upon her form, casting grotesque shadows that writhed like demons in her wake.

The peasants scattered like rats before a flood. Some dove for the corners, others made for the shattered rear entrance, trampling their kin in blind panic. But amidst the chaos, one figure did not move.

A little girl stood in the center of the room, no more than seven years of age.

She clutched the hem of her ragged skirt in tiny fists, her bare feet coated in dust, her wide eyes reflecting the crimson gleam of Kore's gaze. Her voice rose in a whisper that seemed far too calm for the moment.

"They have left me," she said. It was not a question, but a realization—small and cold.

Kore paused.

Her blackened heart, though long calcified by hatred, lurched at the child's words. Something ancient and unspoken stirred beneath her many layers of fury. A memory? A wound?

"Many will," she murmured, her voice a low hymn, soft as ash and heavy with an ageless truth.

Her gaze drifted to the jagged space where the barn doors had once stood, now framing the moonlit path to the forest beyond. The child could still run. Still escape. Still be spared.

Raising a clawed hand, Kore extended one crooked finger. She pressed a thumb—coated in blood, not all of it her own—against the girl's forehead. A flare of searing light blazed for a heartbeat, marking the child with a glyph older than time itself. It burned, but the girl did not flinch.

"Thou art safe from my wraith," Kore intoned. Her voice carried the cadence of a benediction and the weight of a curse. "Take pride in it. Cherish those who are like thee—and those who are not. Do this, and thou shalt never know my wrath."

A single tear traced down Kore's cheek—silver in the torchlight, a relic of a soul she once had and had long since buried beneath centuries of ruin.

The girl nodded. Her tiny lips parted with a simple promise.

"I promise."

Kore said nothing as the child turned and fled, her bare feet silent against the blood-streaked floor. The shadows seemed to part before her, then swallowed her whole as she vanished into the waiting mouth of the forest.

Kore remained still, listening.

She heard the girl's breath, quick and ragged. Heard the rustle of leaves. Heard the wind hush around her tiny form until it was gone.

And then—stillness shattered.

A breath. A whimper. The scrape of a boot. A heartbeat too many.

Kore turned her gaze back to the cowering mass of peasants—their bodies pressed together like insects beneath a stone, sobbing and writhing in the filth of their own cowardice. Her face showed no mercy, no empathy, no second thoughts.

Only judgment.

Her horns pulsed, lengthening as if summoned by the heartbeat of carnage. Their jagged tips gleamed like obsidian.

Her claws spread, twitching with anticipation, with longing.

The fire in her eyes blazed brighter—two orbs of divine judgment, twin suns set to burn a false world down.

Her heart, black as the grave and twice as deep, issued its silent decree.

Slaughter.

* * *

A snarl split the air like a thunderclap, a guttural roar that shattered the fragile silence. The Hunter charged—a hulking mass of sinew, shadow, and hatred, its molten eyes ablaze with bloodlust. Edith braced herself, her breath sharp and cold as forged steel, then unleashed a blinding arc of golden light. The radiant beam lanced through the gloom, searing across the night like the wrath of a vengeful god cast down from the stars.

The creature reeled, its momentum halted by the sheer magnitude of the divine strike. Smoke coiled from its armored hide, thick and pungent, the stench of scorched flesh and smoldering sinew fouling the air. The wind itself recoiled as if offended by the sacrilege.

"Go! Now!" Edith roared, her voice a fierce command laced with urgency and desperation.

The ragged survivors did not hesitate. Driven by raw, primal terror, they stumbled over the bloodstained earth, tripping and clawing their way toward the temple's towering entrance. Fear propelled them like starving dogs chasing salvation. The temple doors gaped wide—an ancient, stone maw yawning to swallow them whole into its sanctified darkness.

The Hunter shuddered. Then, with terrifying swiftness, it twisted to the side, casting off the pain like a beast shedding rain. Its massive tail lashed out—a blur of brutal, raw power—and struck Edith with a sickening force.

The impact lifted her from the ground and hurled her across the valley like a comet torn from heaven. The world spun into a chaotic blur— sky, earth, and the jagged silhouette of the temple blending into a whirlpool of devastation—before she slammed into the dirt, skidding through ruin and rot. A groan clawed its way from her throat as her fingers sank deep into the cracked and dying earth, clawing for anchor in a world crumbling around her.

Then—silence.

The Hunter was gone.

No footsteps. No breath. No rustle of wind nor whisper of wings. Only the erratic drumming of her own pulse and the eerie hush that followed devastation like a shadow.

Her grip on the ground tightened. It was playing with her now. A predator circling the kill, savoring the fear before the final blow.

Edith forced herself upright, every tendon screaming in protest, bones groaning beneath the strain. Running was not an option. The survivors were too frail, too slow. If she left this thing breathing, it would hunt them down one by one, feasting on their terror and peeling them apart like fruit.

No. It ended here.

She closed her eyes and drew a deep, centering breath, exhaling slow and steady. She reached inward, into the stillness beyond thought, where instinct and divine will entwined. The world around her dulled. Sounds faded. The wind carried secrets—tremors in the soil, a subtle shift in pressure, the weight of death gathering its strength once more.

Then—movement.

A whisper of displaced air. A shimmer of shadow. A single breath out of rhythm.

She moved before thought caught up, dropping

into a roll just as the Hunter burst forth from the void. Its claws tore through the space where her neck had been a heartbeat before, the force of its swing splitting the earth with a deafening crack that echoed like judgment.

She twisted mid-air, wings unfurling in a sharp golden flare. The tips caught what little light remained, gleaming like celestial blades. With a surge of power, she launched herself at the beast, her fingers outstretched, talons sharpened to a deadly glint.

She struck.

Her hands found purchase, driving into the beast's face—its flesh like molten armor beneath her golden nails. The creature howled, a shriek that curdled the night, its molten eyes bulging wide with a pain it could not comprehend.

Divine fury ignited within her, coursing through her veins like wildfire. Her limbs surged with raw energy, molten gold spilling through every fiber of her being. Her grip tightened, locking onto the beast's skull as light pulsed from her hands in relentless waves.

"Burn," she whispered, her voice low, cold, absolute.

A torrent of holy radiance erupted outward.

The Hunter shrieked, the sound unraveling from rage to terror, from defiance to something almost human—pleading, afraid. Its skull cracked beneath her grip, bones liquefying, armor melting like wax beneath a dying sun. Flesh boiled. The creature convulsed in its death throes, limbs flailing in a chaotic spasm of desperation.

A final, violent twitch sent Edith flying once more.

She slammed against the temple wall with a bone-jarring crash. The ancient stone cracked beneath her impact, fissures racing outward like lightning. Dust and splinters rained down as she slid to the ground, a cry of pain tearing from her lips. Agony lit up her nerves like an electric storm.

Through the haze, her eyes remained fixed on the broken thing she had slain. The Hunter's headless form writhed for a moment longer, glowing veins flickering erratically, then dimming, fading, finally collapsing into a shattered heap of ruined flesh and armor.

She exhaled, sharp and ragged. It was over.

Or so she thought.

The shadows moved.

Dozens—no, more. Crawling from the periphery of the valley, flickering in the darkness like dying flames. They crept with intent, with hunger. Their eyes glowed with malevolence, embers in a sea of black.

Her pulse quickened. There were more.

Far too many.

And not enough time.

Her gaze snapped toward the temple. The Void-spire Engine—if even one of them still functioned, if even the faintest sliver of power still lingered in those forgotten halls—then hope was not entirely lost.

She staggered to her feet, swallowing the scream that tried to claw its way from her throat.

8

Written in Blood

The forest swallowed them whole. Gnarled branches clawed at the heavens, their skeletal fingers grasping at the thick mist that choked the air. The path ahead was treacherous—narrow and slick with decay, the stench of damp earth mingling with something fouler, something rancid and sweet, like meat left too long in the sun. Talbot led his men in silence, their breaths shallow, their grips tight upon their weapons. They had severed themselves from the main host—a dwindling force sent to their deaths in the blind pursuit of hope. But Talbot was no fool.

Hope did not win wars. Strategy did.

And so, he had devised one.

Kore could not be felled by brute strength alone. If such were possible, she would have perished long before her name became a whispered curse upon dying lips. No, her wretched hide bore no weakness to steel nor fire, and so Talbot sought another answer. Every beast had an origin—a place where it crawled forth from the depths. If they could uncover it—if they could strip away the layers of shadow and deception—perhaps they could unearth the chink in her armor. A fracture. A flaw.

They rode in grim determination, horses wary and snorting, until the trees parted without warning, revealing an unsettling sight.

A cabin.

It stood alone, weathered and lifeless, halfswallowed by the creeping woods. The structure sagged with age, its dark timber warped and swollen by time and moisture. Yet there was no sign of ruin. No rot. No collapsed beams or shattered glass. No clear evidence of habitation— nor of abandonment. It simply was.

"This cannot be it," one of the soldiers muttered, reining his horse to a halt. His voice was edged with disbelief. "A mere dwelling—for such a beast?"

Talbot did not take his eyes from the cabin. His lips pressed into a thin, thoughtful line.

"Thinkest thou it hunts as mere beasts do?" he said at last, his voice low and deliberate. "A wolf slaughters for hunger. A lion, for dominion. But this creature hath no need for flesh, nor kingdom.

It doth not kill to eat, nor to survive. It kills for pleasure. That, above all, doth make it a horror beyond reckoning."

His men exchanged uneasy glances. The forest pressed in closer around them.

"And what then, Captain?" another asked, nudging his mount forward with reluctance. "Shall we burn it?"

"Nay," Talbot replied, swinging down from his saddle. His boots struck the damp earth with a soft thud, the sound muffled by the thick loam. "A blade can slay a man, but knowledge slayeth empires. This place may yield the truth we seek."

With practiced precision, he unfastened his musket from its leather strap, cocking the flint with a sharp click. His sword, sheathed at his hip, felt strangely lighter than it should have—as though steel alone was not enough against the darkness that lay ahead.

He ascended the porch in measured steps, each creak beneath his weight sounding like the groan of something ancient and dying. With a single, purposeful motion, he kicked in the door.

The wood splintered, bursting inward with a deafening crack.

Silence met him.

A silence too deep. Too perfect.

Talbot's jaw tightened. "Show thyself!" he

commanded, his voice cutting through the stifling air like a blade drawn from ice.

Nothing answered.

His men followed close behind, muskets raised, blades unsheathed. Their wary gazes swept the dim interior, scanning corners, rafters, and the dark places where nightmares might dwell.

But the house... was clean.

Too clean.

Dust had not settled upon the wooden surfaces. No cobwebs adorned the beams. The air did not carry the stagnant rot of long neglect. Instead, it was still. Oppressively so. As though the walls themselves were watching. Waiting.

Talbot's eyes narrowed as his gaze fell upon the center of the room—a modest cot, its fabric sunken and damp, as if the weight of something... someone... had pressed upon it for far too long.

"Something is amiss," he muttered, his instincts twisting with unease. This was not the den of a beast. It was something else. Something worse.

His boot shifted.

A sharp clink—metal against metal—sent a jolt through his spine.

He froze.

Lowering his gaze, he spotted it. Nearly hidden beneath a thin layer of dust: a rusted latch set into the floorboards. A trapdoor.

He exhaled slowly, deliberately, like a man about to open a tomb.

"There is more than one," he murmured, his fingers brushing over the latch's cold iron. "And one hath learned to live amongst us."

* * *

"Move! Move!" Edith barked, her wings slicing through the stale air as she crashed into the brittle stone of the temple's atrium, landing hard and bursting into a sprint. The wind from her descent sent dust curling up from long-forgotten cracks in the floor, unsettling the silence that had loomed over this ancient, forsaken place.

The others hesitated—bodies wound tight with uncertainty, eyes darting wildly. Their frantic glances flickered toward the towering doors behind them, still groaning on rusted hinges as they sluggishly heaved shut.

"Where are we going?" one of the refugees gasped, breathless with panic.

"Keep going!" Edith hissed through clenched teeth. There was no time to explain. Her pulse pounded like a war drum in her ears. She threw a desperate look over her shoulder—her gut twisted at the sight of clawed shadows slithering through the widening gaps in the door, monstrous silhouettes stretching hungrily along the temple walls.

The Hunters were coming.

The ragged survivors plunged deeper into the temple's bowels, descending a narrow stone staircase that spiraled into darkness. With each step, the light above dwindled, swallowed by the thick, suffocating air of an ancient crypt untouched for centuries.

By the time they reached the dungeon depths, the world above had vanished into blackness.

Then came the sound.

Above them, the Hunters snarled against the temple doors—a relentless percussion of claw and fang, splintering wood and cracking stone. Their arrival was no longer a question. It was an inevitability.

With a swift motion, Edith raised her hand, and a burst of golden light flared from her forearm, illuminating the chamber. The murky darkness peeled back to reveal a graveyard of failed escape.

Voidspire Engines—ruined, broken, and abandoned husks of machinery—lay scattered like the bones of a long-dead beast. Their spines of twisted steel jutted from the floor, their circuitry stripped bare, their power sources gutted and forgotten.

"They're all destroyed," someone whispered, their voice barely a breath.

A deafening boom rocked the temple from above.

Dust rained down from the ceiling like ash.

The Hunters were getting through.

"There's got to be one operable…" Edith muttered under her breath, desperation coiling in her stomach. Her glowing eyes darted across the wreckage, scanning, hunting—searching for anything that still held the faintest flicker of life. She lunged forward, tearing away rusted plating, her fingers digging through decay.

"We need to go back up!" one of the refugees shrieked, wild with fear. "If we stay, we die!"

Another crash. Louder. Closer. The temple shook with the force of it.

"The only way out is through the machine," Edith snarled, frustration cracking through her voice. "If we don't activate it, this temple becomes our grave."

Her gaze locked onto one engine—its central core dark, but its outer structure mostly intact. She fell upon it, hands working furiously, reassembling what she could, tearing away useless components, fusing pieces that still sparked with potential.

Above them, the thundering of claws on stone grew louder. Closer. A cruel promise of slaughter.

The refugees backed away, terror contorting their faces into masks of helplessness.

"Why isn't it working?!" someone wailed.

And then the truth struck Edith like lightning.

The Kelxsiar hadn't simply abandoned the engines. They hadn't hidden them. They hadn't even bothered to guard them.

They had destroyed them.

Because they couldn't use them.

The Voidspire Engines required something the Kelxsiar could never possess.

Edith tore back the rusted paneling of the control console, revealing a grotesque array of thin, sinewy cables—veins of light long starved. The wires writhed weakly, searching, reaching, desperate to reconnect with what they had been severed from for centuries.

It made sense now.

Only the blood of Par could awaken the Voidspire Engines.

There was no time left to hesitate.

Edith pressed her glowing forearm against the rusted metal, feeling the cold bite of the console against her skin.

The machine reacted at once.

A mechanical shriek ripped through the air as the wires lashed out like living parasites, twisting violently around her arm.

The pain was immediate. Searing. Devouring. Like molten iron pouring through her veins.

She gritted her teeth, stifling a scream as the wires burrowed into her flesh, piercing deep, ravenous for the golden ichor of her bloodline.

Above them, the Hunters let out a synchronized roar. The temple doors had finally given way.

"What's happening?!" one of the refugees cried, peering in horror at the tendrils sinking into Edith's arm.

"My blood," Edith gasped, her voice trembling with agony. "The pure blood of Par. It's the only thing that can revive the machine."

As if in answer, the Voidspire Engine shuddered.

A deep, guttural hum rolled through the chamber—a sound both ancient and powerful, vibrating through the stone, through the very marrow of those who stood near.

Then, it roared to life.

The console burst with golden light. Hollowed machinery surged awake, flooding the chamber with a radiance so intense it rivaled the fires of a dying sun.

Above, the Hunters froze mid-charge, their eyes wide, reflecting the blinding glow of rebirth.

Edith collapsed to her knees, gasping. Her arm was a ruin—etched with golden streaks, veins of celestial energy burning just beneath the surface where the machine had fed from her.

She had done it.

She had awakened the engine.

And in doing so, she had written the tale of escape in her own blood.

The hatch groaned open beneath Talbot's grip, the wooden frame rotted with time, its hinges rusted like the bones of the long-forgotten dead. A damp, putrid breath of air exhaled from the underground compartment, thick with the scent of earth and decay. The lantern's glow barely touched the depths below, swallowed whole by an abyss that did not belong to this world.

One of the soldiers stepped forward, his musket aimed downward into the gaping maw of the cellar. His breath hitched at the sight of the grotesque symbols carved into the walls—twisted spirals of ink, their sharp, unnatural angles forming impossible shapes. The words bled from the stone as though the walls themselves were alive, weeping black scripture.

"What Devil's tongue is this?" the soldier murmured, his knuckles whitening around the stock of his rifle.

Talbot descended first, his boots striking the dirt floor with a muted thud. His eyes scanned the markings, and a chill crept along his spine. He dragged his fingers across the paint—flaking with age yet still feeling wet, as though the ink had only just dried.

"This is not of this world," he muttered under his breath, his voice carrying an eerie finality.

His fingers traced a series of grotesque figures, monstrous effigies coiling in reverence around a central form—a hulking entity, its jagged wings unfurled, horns spiraling like a crown, its hands stretched outward as though beckoning dominion over all things. The image throbbed with implied purpose, as if painted with intent too ancient to fathom.

A sudden, deafening *pop* cracked through the air, reverberating through the hollow of the cabin. It was distant, yet unnatural—not the sharp ring of musket fire, nor the thunderous boom of artillery— but something else. Something older.

A sound like bones snapping in reverse.

Talbot's breath caught. He knew this was it.

"It's coming from outside."

They stormed up from the trapdoor with haste, emerging into the bitter chill of the night. The wet air hung heavy with the scent of damp wood and something fouler—something acrid, like flesh burned in a way it was never meant to be.

Talbot's grip tightened around his rifle, his pulse a roaring drumbeat in his ears. His men followed close behind, their bodies wound tight with antici- pation, the weight of God's justice in their hands and the certainty of their own mortality etched into their hearts.

And then they saw it.

The very fabric of reality stretched thin before them, warping like a glass pane struck by a slow-moving hammer. Veins of darkness spread through the sky like cracks into oblivion. The moonlight twisted, bending away from the disturbance, as though light itself refused to acknowledge what was happening.

And from that abyss, something fell.

No—*not* fell.

Descended.

Figures emerged, one first, landing in the dirt with a weight that defied the delicate grace of its form.

Talbot had never seen anything like it before, and yet, somehow, his instinct knew *exactly* what it was.

Wings. White as the clouds of Heaven.

"SIGHT IN!" Talbot bellowed, his voice cracking like a whip across the night.

The soldiers snapped their rifles up in unison, fingers taut on the triggers, their fear barely caged by discipline.

The figure before them rose to its full height, and Talbot found himself staring into the face of something not quite angel, not quite man—but *something* other.

Her golden skin shimmered beneath the moon,

unmarred and radiant. Her wings—too perfect, too unnatural—shifted as though adjusting to the weight and air of a world that did not belong to her. Her eyes, sharp and unwavering, swept over the barrels of their rifles without fear.

She had seen war before.

She was not afraid of them.

"We mean you no harm."

Her voice was steady, unwavering. She was not pleading.

And Talbot noticed something else—something subtle but unmistakable.

She spoke differently. The way she carried herself. The accent, the dialect—it had changed.

"Give me one reason why I should not fire upon thee, creature," Talbot spat, his breath heavy with wariness, every word a warning drawn tight with tension.

She did not flinch. She did not blink.

"If I meant to harm thee," she said, her voice a blade of certainty, "thou wouldst already be dead."

Her calmness unnerved him more than any snarl, any threat, any scream.

"Your kind," Talbot pressed, his voice rising, rage and fear battling for dominion over his soul. "One with wings black as a demon haunts our lands. Slaughters our people. Innocents—women, children—dead, ripped apart as beasts are wont to do. Art thou kin to this devil?"

She hesitated.

Talbot saw it—a flicker of something. Pain.

Her jaw tensed. Her hands curled into fists.

"Kore," she whispered.

A name.

Talbot gritted his teeth. "Who is she?"

A deep breath followed, as if she were swallowing something unspeakable.

"She is my sister," she finally said.

A bitter silence fell between them, thick with tension and unspoken horrors.

Talbot's heart pounded like war drums heralding an imminent charge.

"Who art thou?" he demanded.

The question hung in the air like a blade poised at a throat.

For a moment, she did not answer.

Then, as if severing something within herself, she spoke.

"I am Ara, of Par."

Talbot felt the name settle like a weight upon his soul. It felt old. Heavy. Sacred. Cursed.

"And I will help thee slay my sister."

9

Slay Thy KIN

The scent of burning pine lingered in the rafters of the weather-beaten cabin, mingling with sweat, dried blood, and the earthy musk of the forest that surrounded them. Moonlight strained through crooked planks in the roof, laying fractured silver across the floor where warriors and strangers stood shoulder to shoulder—Par refugees, half-dead villagers, and the last surviving soldiers of Talbot's militia.

Ara stood near the hearth, her golden eyes gleaming like ancient suns through the dim light. Her posture was rigid, a sentinel bearing the weight of divine blood and cursed lineage alike.

Kleiad broke the silence, stepping forward with hesitation flickering behind his eyes.

"You want us to do what?" he said, his tone edged with panic. "We're not fighters, Ara. Most of us don't even have weapons. And you want us to help stop that thing?"

The others turned toward him—some confused, some afraid, all weary from days of loss and horrors none of them were trained to face.

Ara's expression did not shift. She met Kleiad's gaze with quiet, solemn gravity.

"Aye. I would ask thy strength—not as soldiers, but as souls who have endured. If she returneth, one among thee must remain behind… to stall her, if only for moments. That moment may buy us salvation."

Tension rippled through the crowd like a chill wind slipping beneath woolen cloaks. Kleiad looked around, disbelieving.

"That's suicide."

Ara turned her attention to a cloaked figure in the corner.

"Thou," she said. "I know thy kind. I see the lines upon thy skin—Nerl-born, art thou not? Thou hast suffered greatly, but I say to thee, thy suffering is not thy shame. The curse that hath befallen thy people came not of sin, but from war."

The cloaked figure stirred. A pale hand rose and slowly drew back the hood.

The room dimmed slightly, as though the very shadows acknowledged her presence.

Her skin glimmered faintly with dull, bioluminescent veins—the glow once radiant, now faded like a dying star. Her eyes, dimmed by time and torment, met Ara's with a flicker of reluctant recognition.

"What name dost thou bear?" Ara asked softly.

The Nerl nodded. "Crauo," she whispered, her voice hoarse, the name more a memory than a claim.

"Crauo… if Kore descendeth again upon this place, thou must reach us. Warn us. Send thy message on winds or shadows—I care not how. Only let us know. I trust thee."

A rustle passed through the group like dry leaves shifting underfoot, uncertainty stirring in the hearts of the gathered.

Talbot, standing near the door with musket in hand, shifted uneasily.

"And what wouldst thou have of us?"

Ara met his gaze without blinking.

"Thou and thy men shall patrol on horseback. Keep watch for sign or sound. I shall fly above, my eyes stretched beyond thine own. We will not be caught unawares."

Talbot frowned, his jaw clenched tightly beneath his beard.

"And what maketh thee so certain thou canst stop her?"

Ara's voice dropped to a grave hush.

"She is of mine own blood. Her wrath is mine. Her strength… and her weakness. I know her."

* * *

The hooves of Talbot's horse thundered against the softened earth. The forest around them was silent—too silent. Even the owls had abandoned the branches.

He peered upward. Ara was a pale silhouette in the clouds above, her wings spread wide, casting brief shadows over the troop like some ghostly watchman from a forgotten heaven.

"I know not if I sin in doing this," Talbot muttered, gripping his reins tighter. "Mayhap we ride beside the Devil herself."

One of the younger soldiers—green-eyed and pale, barely grown into his armor—chimed in with nervous conviction.

"They are not demons, sir. Merely creatures we know not. Like beasts of some distant isle, never before charted."

Talbot exhaled sharply, eyes narrowing as he scanned the moonlit path ahead.

"Is it the Lord's will we discover them… or that they discover us?"

They passed through one, then two empty villages. Bodies lay in frozen poses of anguish, twisted by claws and fire, remnants of families torn asunder beneath blackened skies.

At last, Talbot raised his hand.

"Hold."

The troop slowed, dust trailing from their horses' hooves like fading smoke.

Ara descended like a shadow peeled from the sky, her feet barely making a sound as she landed beside them.

"Why stoppest thou?" she asked, her eyes already scanning the dead town with grim precision.

"Our beasts tire. As do we." Talbot removed his hat, wiping the sweat from his brow. "No soldier can fight well with lungs like bellows and legs like sticks."

"Kore's fury hath no need for rest," Ara countered, her tone hard with urgency.

But before she could press further, a rustle broke the silence.

Every soldier turned, muskets raised. Ara's hand ignited with radiant fire, its light casting long, flickering shadows over their wary faces.

From the blackened woods stumbled a blood-drenched woman—barefoot, shaking, her clothes torn and caked with mud and ash.

"My children," she rasped, her eyes wild. "They… they were taken. Slain. All of them."

Talbot leapt down and caught her before she

collapsed into the mud.

"Who did this?" he demanded. "Speak, woman!"

"It came from the shadows," she cried, trembling violently. "And it wore the night like a cloak. Red eyes. Black wings."

Ara's chest tightened. Her gaze hardened, burning with a terrible resolve.

"How didst thou survive?" she asked coldly.

The woman's eyes flicked to Ara. Wide. Unblinking. Empty.

"She let me live… perhaps… perhaps to tell thee."

Talbot turned to Ara, alarm flickering behind his stern demeanor.

"We must take her to thy dwelling, else she shall perish before dawn."

Ara clenched her jaw, resisting the frustration building within her chest.

"Kore is close. Every moment we dally brings her closer still."

"If we break, we shatter. Let us mend first," Talbot countered. "There shall be no hunt if thy allies be corpses."

Ara looked to the forest, her golden eyes catching the flicker of something just beyond the trees.

Something watching.

Something waiting.

She exhaled, the air thick with coming blood.

"Very well. We ride—but not back to our hovel.

There is another ruin, north of here. We make for that."

Talbot extended a hand to the trembling woman.

"Come with us. We shall see thee safe… for as long as breath still fills our lungs."

* * *

The air inside the cabin sat heavy, like the stillness before a thunderstorm. It was the kind of silence that made men glance over their shoulders without knowing why, a breathless anticipation that coiled in the lungs and refused to let go.

Talbot knelt beside the hearth, reaching into his battered satchel and withdrawing a hard wedge of black bread. It was stale—nearly stone—but it would sustain. He extended it toward the woman whose tattered shift still clung to her bloodstained skin like a shroud. Her face, pale beneath streaks of ash and crimson, turned toward him, but her eyes—strangely distant—did not blink, as if she gazed into a fire only she could see.

She raised a trembling hand and pushed the food away with a ghostly wave.

"If thou refuseth to eat," Talbot murmured, returning the bread to his satchel, "then shall thy strength fail thee when battle draweth nigh. And battle shall draw nigh, I swear it."

The woman's gaze remained fixed on the flickering hearth, its flame mirrored faintly in her hollow eyes.

"And how dost thou plan to kill it?" she asked, her voice hollow as an old grave, its echo swallowed by the soot-dark rafters.

Talbot opened his mouth, but before the first word escaped, Ara stepped forward. Her presence was immediate—divine light dimmed by dread, a heavenly being grown weary of heaven. Her golden eyes burned low, not with rage, but with grim resolve.

"We shall not kill her," Ara said flatly.

A silence as heavy as iron cloaked the room. The soldiers stiffened where they stood, hands tightening on their muskets. Talbot turned slowly, his brow furrowed deep with disbelief.

"If I mistake not," he began, his voice slow with measured incredulity, "the plan was to slay the beast. Was it not thy very tongue that urged us to ride in arms?"

Ara met his stare unflinchingly, her expression carved in stone.

"Aye. But know this now: none of us shall slay her. Not with blade, nor powder, nor God's own wrath."

A soldier stepped forward, voice flaring hot with contempt.

"Thou seek'st to spare her. She is thy blood, I warrant, but she hath drowned this land in murder. Dost thou now wish to clasp hands with death?"

"I wish to end her wrath," Ara replied, her voice unshaken, steady as a vow. "And I shall. But not by murder. I will cast her down and bind her. Her hand shall spill no more blood."

"And what giveth thee such certainty?" asked the woman. Her voice cracked like dried parchment as she wiped at her tear-streaked face. A sliver of skin peeled away beneath her fingers—unnatural, curling like scorched vellum.

Ara's eyes narrowed, tracking every movement.

"She is mine own sister," Ara said, her voice suddenly quieter, wearier. "We hath endured much—together and apart. I have fought her… and I failed. Yet I rise again, with truth upon my lips."

Talbot's eyes narrowed. His knuckles whitened where they gripped the strap of his musket.

"What truth speakest thou of?"

Ara's hands tightened at her sides. The firelight caught her profile, casting it in streaks of gold and blood.

"Kore is cursed," she whispered. "Her crimson skin and blackened wings are not her sin—they are our father's. Long ago, he did wage war 'gainst the Nerl, a folk of magic deep and wild. In his pride, he slaughtered them… and they, in turn, laid a curse on his blood. It struck not me, but her. She was born blighted for his crimes."

The woman trembled. Her lips parted slightly, as if the wind itself had touched her nerves and left them raw. Talbot stepped closer, suspicion flaring in his gaze like kindling catching fire.

"Art thou well?" he asked, voice cautious.

And then—

A slough of skin peeled away from the woman's cheek, revealing a raw, glistening crimson beneath. The glow of the hearth danced grotesquely upon it.

Talbot recoiled.

"By God!" he hissed, scrambling backward, reaching for his flintlock. "The beast! She hath taken the form of woman!"

Another soldier cried out, voice breaking with alarm.

"Deceiver! Witch! She's upon us!"

Before Ara could act, a pulse of voidfire erupted from the woman's chest, ripping through the cabin like a thunderclap made flesh. The blast flung soldiers like ragdolls, shattering wood, bone, and beam. The roof groaned above them, then collapsed inward with a deafening crash.

Kore stood revealed.

Her black wings unfurled like the sails of death, spanning nearly the width of the broken room. Her skin burned crimson in the dim light, her long, wet hair clinging to her cheeks like shadowed vines. Her presence filled the room with dread so thick it strangled breath.

She descended like a hammer, slamming Ara to the floor with an impact that shattered stone and shook the very bones of the world. Her claws dug into her sister's scalp, pressing her skull into the dirt-streaked floorboards.

"Thou knewest!" Kore howled, her voice a dirge of fury that shook the rafters. "Thou traitorous worm! **THOU KNEWEST!**"

Ara writhed beneath her, choking on pain and dust, her wings twitching beneath the weight.

"I did not—I learned it from a prisoner! A Nerl, freed by mine own hand!"

Kore's lip curled. Her eyes glowed like coals in a furnace, her breath a sickly heat.

"Thinkest thou I care for his crimes?! Nay! I care not for our father, for his throne, nor for his failures!" She leaned down, her mouth close to Ara's ear, her breath scorching. "But know this—I found a Nerl. A living one. I spared it. I smelled its cursed blood… in our home."

Ara's eyes widened with dawning horror.

"Kore… what hast thou done?"

Kore's grin widened—cracked and unholy.

"I shall finish what he began. Not for his glory…

but for mine."

And with that, she hurled Ara like a javelin through the shattered wall of the cabin. The divine warrior burst through bark and branch, her body breaking trunks like brittle reeds until she finally skidded to a ragged stop, buried half in soil at the forest's edge.

A heavy silence followed, thick and final.

Until the trees began to whisper again.

Until the darkness breathed her name.

* * *

"Nay… nay! Dear God, nay!" Ara cried, clawing her way from the smoldering heap of broken earth and splintered wood that had buried her like a corpse in waiting. Her voice, hoarse and trembling, tore through the stillness of the ravaged forest like a blade drawn across tender flesh.

The soil fell from her wings in sodden clumps as they burst outward with a crack of radiant light, their divine plumage tattered but not yet broken. With a single, powerful beat, she soared skyward—ascending like a wounded angel fleeing the grave. Her form tore through the mist-heavy clouds, each passing second blurring the heavens into streaks of grey and crimson.

Her breath came in ragged pulls. Her ribs ached.

The pain mattered not.

Beneath her, the world was dying.

Ara pushed faster. Her wings cut the air like drawn swords, slicing through gust and gale. She flew with fury, with desperation—but also with fear. A fear she dared not name. A war waged within her chest: the part that still knew her sister, and the part that now feared her.

Was she too late? Had Kore outwitted her—again? Had her madness already reached the helpless? The prisoners Ara had sworn to protect?

"Sweet Christ preserve them," Ara muttered, her eyes scanning the scarred horizon. The sun dipped low, bleeding into the clouds like a cauterized wound. The sky was stained with the hue of a world coming undone.

Her heart thundered louder than the wind.

In the distance, the black smoke of fire curled like the fingers of the dead. The temple spires that once pierced the heavens now lay fractured—gnarled bones of a sacred corpse. She could feel the scent of death—tangible, bitter, and familiar. Her soul recoiled from it, yet she pressed on.

Ara's descent from the heavens bore no grace. Her wings, battered and begrudging, surrendered her to a glide more mournful than measured. She touched down amid the ashen bones of what had once been sanctuary—a cabin, humble in frame yet sacred in memory. Now it lay torn asunder, its timber ribs snapped, its hearth gutted and blackened, the air thick with the perfume of ruin and smoke. The home she once shared with Kore—sister, kin, and curse—had been desecrated into a relic of ash and grief.

The silence was not silent. It breathed. Groaned. Wept through the broken boards and curled stones. Ara's boots sank into the scorched soil as she moved forward, her breath sharp with dread. A whisper rustled the hush—a stir too deliberate to be mere wind. She turned, swift as lightning, and her gaze caught the shimmer of something unnatural pooled upon the ground.

A trail. Not of water, nor ichor, but a glowing, pulsing thread—silver-gold like starlight spilled from a broken soul. Nerl blood.

Ara knelt, her fingers trembling as they hovered above the radiant trail. The smell was faintly sweet, laced with a sorrow older than Par itself. She followed the glittering path like a thread of prophecy, until she came upon what remained of Crauo.

The Nerl lay twisted among the ruin, her once-glowing lines dimmed, her form riven and gashed as if torn by the claws of the abyss. Yet even in her shattered state, she lived.

"She turned Kleiad to…" Crauo choked, coughing up a shimmer that stained her lips with dying light. "Reduced him to ashes."

"God's mercy…" Ara breathed, kneeling beside her. "I am sorry, child. This I did not foresee."

"No—listen to me," Crauo hissed. Her voice was strained but clear, sharp as shattered glass. "You can't just stop her. You have to kill her. There are others—more of us, scattered across this realm. She's going to hunt them. I could feel it. It was in her mind—pure, concentrated malice."

Ara shook her head, grief clashing with resistance. "She is mine own blood—my soul's twin. I cannot—"

"I don't care who she is," Crauo snapped, her glowing eyes boring into Ara's. "You have to do what your father couldn't. She won't stop. I felt it, in the marrow of her thoughts. You don't kill her, and we all die."

A faint hum stirred the air. Crauo's bloodied hand lifted—weak but deliberate—and a streak of light uncoiled from her palm, a sliver of energy like the breath of dying stars. It shot forward and struck Ara's brow, sinking into her mind like molten revelation.

The vision seized her: a location etched into her thoughts—a sacred place, veiled in crimson dusk and towering stones. The last known refuge of the scattered Nerl. Kore was headed there. And if she reached it…

Ara's wings exploded outward, luminous and wrathful, a thunderous pulse of force rippling through the trees. Leaves were torn from branches. Birds scattered in panic. The very air recoiled as she took flight, soaring upward like a divine arrow loosed from the bow of fate.

Her heart pounded with fire.

She had delayed this reckoning far too long. The truth had always waited for her at the end of this path. The cruel irony carved itself into her soul— her father had birthed a scourge, and now she must become the blade.

The wind tore at her face. Her eyes narrowed. Her fists clenched tight, light pulsing between her fingers.

"Forgive me, sister…" she whispered to the screaming winds.

Then she vanished into the sky, trailing fire and fury in her wake.

Only a few hours had waned since Ara had taken to the skies, yet time—as it often does in moments of dread—had felt stretched thin and fragile. The weight of urgency coiled in her chest like a serpent. She soared now over the treetops, their once-proud boughs appearing shrunken and brittle, as if

Par itself recoiled from the horrors it had birthed.

Her wings dipped, catching the ash-laden wind as she descended into a vast and blistered stretch of forest. At first glance, all lay quiet—too quiet. But stillness was often the mouth of catastrophe.

Ara touched down lightly, her sandals pressing into scorched earth, her senses prickling with unease. Around her, the trees whispered with the silence of the damned. Her gaze swept the clearing—until her eyes caught a corruption of nature. The brush was melted in jagged, glassy swathes, the soil charred to obsidian slag. The air stank of smoke, rot, and scorched blood.

Her heart thudded. Nay… too late.

The trail was there—a path of death cut into the forest. Blackened foliage. Trampled roots. And then the telltale shimmer of Nerl blood, like scattered stardust spilled in grief. It glimmered faintly along the ground, leading her deeper into the gloom.

And then—"H–help…" came a brittle voice, cracked like ancient stone.

Ara turned, her eyes locking onto a trembling hand lifted feebly from the forest floor. She rushed forward, her breath catching in her throat. A Nerl being—his glowing veins dimmed, his flesh riven and rent—lay twisted in a pool of his own bioluminescence.

"It's you…" the being rasped. "We never wanted war."

"Nor did I," Ara whispered, falling to her knees. "I am not mine father. I sought not to follow his sins."

"It's too late. Maybe it was always going to happen," the Nerl muttered, blood streaming from his lips like liquefied moonlight.

"Please, I came to save thee. Believe me—I meant to stop her."

The Nerl's breath grew labored, his eyes twitching weakly. "Kill it. Kill the evil that remains from your father. You want to fix this? End her."

Ara's voice broke. "I shall restrain her, imprison her if fate demands it—but slay her? I cannot. She is mine blood… and I love her still."

"Well," the Nerl breathed, gaze hardening with the final shreds of will, "then you've doomed this world. She won't stop. She's past reason."

And before Ara could respond, a vice closed around the back of her neck.

She was yanked upward—flung like a rag doll—until the air was torn from her lungs, and her limbs dangled in the wind. Kore had her.

"Thou dost choose them?" Kore bellowed, her voice a shriek of unholy thunder. "These witless wretches—these carrion-eaters who crawled from the filth of ash? Thou wouldst have them over me?!"

Her hand burned against Ara's throat—hot as iron fresh from the forge. Ara coughed, twisted, kicked herself free, and with a cry of fury, her wings burst outward in a radiant shockwave, shattering Kore's hold.

The air erupted as Ara shot upward, her hands blazing with divine light.

"I begged thee to cease! But now, sister—thou leavest me no choice!"

Kore laughed—a hideous, hollow thing. "Then draw thy blade, holy thing. And bleed with the wretches thou dost protect."

Ara's hands clapped together, unleashing a beam of golden force, pure and searing. But Kore twisted—inhuman in her speed—and carved through the air with her claws, raking a gash across Ara's chest. Blood sprayed like droplets of starlight.

Ara reeled, tumbling—but not falling. She steadied in air, fury igniting in her heart.

Her wings unfurled wider, their edges sharpening. Armor forged of raw light began to manifest along her arms and legs, crystalline plates shaped by bloodline power. Golden claws extended from the tips of her wings. Her eyes burned, then shifted—gold to electric blue. The sky dimmed as her voice split the heavens.

A roar of divinity.

Kore answered.

Her wings were monstrous, now bristling with bone-like talons. Her horns stretched backward, blackened and cracked like volcanic stone, her red skin pulsing with arcane lightning. Her eyes were twin maelstroms of crimson fury, leaking power with each blink.

The sisters collided midair—light and darkness crashing with the roar of worlds ending.

Golden brilliance met crimson lightning in a violent shockwave that splintered the clouds, sent trees shuddering, and cracked the earth below. The collision blinded the forest in searing flashes, the impact booming like divine artillery.

They fell.

Twin stars cast from heaven—plummeting toward the forest canopy. Branches shattered. Bark exploded. Dust and blood showered the dying trees as they crashed through limbs and foliage, their bodies colliding with the ground like thunder made flesh.

The forest groaned.

The world held its breath.

* * *

Ara lay still, half-buried in the bruised soil, her chest heaving with shallow, ragged breaths. The earth beneath her trembled as Kore descended like a harbinger of annihilation, her form a blur of wings and wrath. Without pause, without mercy, Kore struck—a flurry of thunderous haymakers that cracked Ara's ribs and cratered the ground with each devastating blow. Bones splintered. The forest shuddered. Leaves scattered like frightened birds fleeing the roar of a coming storm.

Blood trailed down Ara's lips as she lifted her head, her eyes clouded with pain, her vision swimming in red and shadow. Her sister loomed above her—fury incarnate—eyes glowing with a malevolent fire that seemed to burn with the heat of a fallen star.

"I have no sister," Kore snarled, her voice a guttural rasp, trembling with betrayal and centuries of suppressed loathing.

She raised her burning hand, pulsing with infernal energy, ready to deliver the final, obliterating blow—when, like the wrath of a vengeful god, the roots of the forest erupted around her.

Gnarled tendrils shot up from the soil, ancient and sentient, wrapping around Kore's arm with the strength of a dozen wolves. She shrieked as the roots pulled taut—then tighter still—until, with a nauseating pop, her arm snapped at the elbow, bone jutting like broken ivory through her skin.

Her scream split the air like a cleaver.

More roots surged forth, coiling around her limbs, her spine, her wings, dragging her back like prey toward the forest's final judgment. Her form twisted unnaturally, bones crunching beneath the relentless force of nature's vengeance. The sound was sickening—a symphony of tendons snapping, of ligaments tearing, of muscle unraveling beneath the ancient will of the grove. Her wrath gave way to terror.

Ara's gaze shifted—and locked with the one responsible: a lone, broken Nerl slumped against the base of the glowing tree, his arm extended in silent command. Blood soaked the ground beneath him, pooling around his knees, but power pulsed visibly from his will—resolute and unwavering.

"Strike now! End her!" the Nerl demanded, his voice ragged but filled with unyielding purpose. "You will never have another chance."

Tears blurred Ara's vision. Her legs shook beneath her. She summoned what strength remained and formed a blade of pure light in her hand—its radiance humming like a divine whisper, trembling in tune with the chaos in her heart. She stepped forward, trembling, staring down at the heaving chest of the monster that had once been her sister.

One thrust. One motion. That was all it would take to end this.

The blade quivered in her grip.

"I cannot," she whispered, her voice cracking under the unbearable weight of memory and love. The blade dissolved into radiant dust. Her arms fell uselessly to her sides.

The Nerl's face hardened, bitterness carved into every line.

"So be it," he muttered.

With a cry that rippled through the bones of the forest, the Nerl cast his final spell. His eyes ignited with red fire as he poured the last of his essence into the earth. The roots responded at once—shuddering with eldritch hunger. Scarlet tendrils of cursed energy pulled from Kore's body, winding outward like bloody threads—from her eyes, her open wounds, her gasping mouth. She screamed as the power was ripped away, her defiance shattered into agony.

The black of her wings disintegrated into ash. Her horns withered like charred wood. Her crimson flesh faded, gradually returning to gold as the cursed M.E.P.S. mutagen was siphoned from her body like venom from an infected wound.

At last, her body collapsed—limp, breath shallow, no-longer cursed, though barely clinging to life.

Ara stumbled forward, hands aglow with trembling energy. She conjured a cocoon of brilliant, humming light, its sacred aura pulsing with celestial resonance. It enveloped Kore's broken form, sealing her in a stasis of divine imprisonment. The roots, recognizing the cocoon's power, unwrapped with reverence, releasing their shattered captive to the mercy of divine containment.

Silence returned to the grove—heavy, sacred, final—broken only by Ara's labored breathing.

The tree beside them pulsed with unnatural light. Its bark was veined with glowing threads—eldritch and alive. It throbbed with power now, no longer just a relic but a living prison, a beacon and a warning.

"She is liberated from the curse," the Nerl said, his voice weak, barely more than breath. He was pale as moonlight, his skin drawn tight over bone. "So long as this tree remain guarded, she shall not reclaim her wrath. But fail to protect it…" His eyes found Ara's. "And her power will return… and so shall her hate."

Ara turned slowly toward the glowing cocoon. Her hand trembled as it hovered in the air. Her heart felt heavier than it ever had before, thick with grief, guilt, and uncertainty.

The Nerl's gaze lingered on her with fading intensity. "If you can't kill her… who will?"

$$10$$

Grace

Talbot sat hunched upon the stiff cot within the infirmary tent, its canvas walls sagging beneath the weight of death and despair. The rank scent of blood, sweat, and bitter herbs clung to the air like a funeral shroud, heavy and inescapable. His garments, tattered and soiled, hung limp upon a frame carved by war and woe, each movement betraying the toll of battles fought not only with weapons, but with the soul.

Fresh bandages swathed his brow, stained through with blood that refused to dry—just as the horrors etched in his memory refused to fade. A sharp ache pulsed behind his eyes with every heartbeat, a constant reminder that survival carried its own kind of torment.

He did not speak. He merely breathed, slow and shallow, as though each inhalation required permission from a higher court of Heaven. The silence pressed in, thick and sacred, broken only by the distant groans of the wounded and the whispered prayers of nurses tending to the broken.

Then, the flap of the tent parted.

Bootsteps approached—heavy, measured, deliberate. Each step struck the earth with the certainty of command. In stepped a man of station, clad in the polished buff coat and gorget of a high-ranking officer. His presence was crisp against the gloom, his uniform unmarred by ash or blood. The leather of his gauntlets bore the creases of long campaigns, and his boots bore the mud of many fields, yet his face remained composed, untouched by the filth of the day.

He bore the quiet weight of command like a mantle of iron.

"None e'er said the field of Mars was a place of ease," said the man, his voice deep and grave, as though shaped by the winds of war and the burden of command.

Talbot made to rise, his movements slow, pained, each gesture a battle in its own right—but the officer raised a hand, halting him.

"Peace, Captain," the man spoke. "Hold thy post."

"Captain Weaver," Talbot rasped, settling back onto the cot with a wince. "I take it thou comest for the debriefing... though my thoughts be as muddled as the Devil's mire. My skull yet rings from the blow."

"Nay," said Captain Weaver, drawing a stool and resting upon it with the ease of a man who had sat beside too many dying soldiers. "Not for chart nor tally am I come, but for thy soul's reckoning. Mortal men were ne'er meant to see the things thou hast seen. And yet… thou livest. With breath still in thy chest, and blood yet warm in thy veins."

"By the Lord's hand," Talbot murmured, his voice hoarse as a funeral dirge. "No other power preserved me. I… I believe He did send down an angel. A guardian, cloaked in fire and glory."

Captain Weaver's brow furrowed—not with doubt, but with the weight of contemplation. "Others have said much the same. Talk of wings, of light… of beings not born of this world. Some call them miracles."

Talbot's lips twitched—whether into a smile or a grimace, it was impossible to tell. "Miracles," he echoed. "I had thought thou wouldst call them fiends, as the others have."

Weaver let forth a short chuckle, dry as dust from a forgotten crypt. "Aye, some might. But miracles oft come dressed in robes of terror. And by my reckoning, one such saved thy life."

Talbot nodded slowly. "That she did."

Weaver's gaze darkened, like the sky before a

storm. "Yet our time to hunt such beings is scant. The wars of men wait not for angels."

Talbot's head turned, his battered eyes rising to meet the captain's with a flicker of defiant resolve—something hard and enduring that had survived the fire.

"There is no our, Captain."

Weaver blinked, caught off guard. "Speak clear."

"I shall find them," Talbot said, his voice steadier now, like stone being reforged beneath the hammer. "All of them. Whether creature of Heaven or horror from the stars, I shall seek them out. For good or ill, I am marked. And I can scarce abide a world wherein such forces walk unseen."

Silence settled between them once more, this time heavier—thicker than the canvas around them, deeper than the wounds either man could name. It lingered like fog before Weaver finally answered, his voice low and solemn:

"Then God go with thee, Talbot. For thou treadest a path no soldier was trained to walk."

Talbot's grip tightened on the edge of his cot, fingers white with the pressure of purpose.

"I walk it still."

III

The New World

*We are warriors of Par, our blood golden
and everlasting.
Fathers, sons, and brothers—entry to the
Vast Sea is won through death in battle.
Mothers, daughters, and sisters—entry is
granted through the bearing of those who
perish in battle.
Par endures, so long as we endure.*
Velaris

11

Decorated

ENTURIES LATER

The morning sky stretched overhead in a blanket of gunmetal gray, pulled taut across the polished parade grounds like a storm cloud held hostage by unseen hands. A cold wind swept across the flat expanse, its icy fingers biting at regulation collars and gleaming brass fixtures, yet the cadence thundered on—boots striking pavement in perfect, unbroken synchronicity, every stomp echoing across the valley like the ritual drumbeat of an ancient war.

"Left! Left! Left, right, left!"

The voice that commanded them was fierce—unnatural in tone. It was not by sheer volume or authority that it dominated the grounds, but by its very presence. It hummed with something older than the earth itself, something eternal. It demanded obedience not through fear or rank, but through gravity, like the pull of a distant star whose light had traveled through millennia solely to shine upon this singular moment.

At the side of the formation stood a woman who had not aged in eons—though she bore the camouflage of time with uncanny perfection.

Dressed in the pristine formality of Marine Corps Dress Blues, her chest bore more ribbons than any living service member—decorations won in battles forgotten by history, earned in conflicts waged by nations whose names had crumbled into dust. Gold piping traced the seams of her jacket with quiet authority, while blood-red stripes blazed down the sides of her navy trousers, bold and unforgiving as war wounds. Her white cover sat perfectly atop golden-blonde hair, hair untouched by time, fatigue, or sorrow.

She was Master Gunnery Sergeant Edith Guzman, or so the records proclaimed. But in truth, she was Ara—the celestial daughter of a shattered realm. The last sentinel of a bloodline cursed by gods and damned by unending war. Time had made her a ghost in plain sight, hidden behind the mask of medals and the armor of discipline. And the world—blinded by its politics, its machines, and its endless bloodletting—never once looked deeply enough to see her for what she truly was.

"Platoon—halt!" she barked, the syllables sharp and clean, striking the air like polished steel.

The column stopped instantly, with textbook precision—heels locked, rifles snapped into position, eyes forward. The silence that followed was perfect, unbroken. Sacred. Edith—Ara—surveyed them with a solemn gaze, her eyes sweeping across the young faces standing at rigid attention. Some were fresh and unmarked, barely out of high school. Others bore the hollow stares of men who had already glimpsed the edge of death and returned bearing invisible scars.

She had trained thousands like them across countless generations. Watched them rise, fight, fall, and be forgotten by the living. She bore their memories in silence, stacking them like tombstones behind her steady, impassive stare.

There was a peace to be found in this ritual. In the structure. In the discipline. In the cold comfort of orders obeyed and duties fulfilled. Here, there were no mobs with torches, no superstitious whispers in the dark, no celestial wars raging unseen above their heads. Here there were only ranks, reasons, and rules—a simpler kind of battlefield. And in that, she had found something resembling peace.

And yet…

In the deepest corridors of her mind, she still felt it—the faintest tremor, like the vibration of a bowstring long since loosed, but still singing. The distant hum of a storm that had not passed, only been imprisoned.

Her sister.

The memory was carved into her soul like a brand. Kore—trapped in a tomb of luminous energy beneath a forgotten, glowing tree. A cocoon not simply of light, but of sorrow and guilt. It pulsed still, hidden somewhere far beyond the grasp of mortal armies and mechanized death, nestled in the secret folds of a world that had learned to forget its oldest nightmares.

It was a reminder of power—of what power became when it festered, when it mourned, when it hated.

A punishment that had become a prayer.

And though Ara had clothed herself in discipline and silence, she felt it again now—a flicker, a tug deep in her blood, faint but undeniable.

As if the coffin itself had begun to groan in its sleep.

* * *

The lights inside the battalion office buzzed low, a dull electric hum beneath the heavy silence that surrounded her. Edith stood at the window, her eyes fixed on the drill field beyond—its rigid lines etched into the frost-laced earth like scars carved deep into memory. Recruits moved in practiced formation, boot heels biting into the dirt in rhythm. The cadence echoed from their lungs like the distant ghosts of old wars, filling the air with a solemn kind of music.

Her gaze drifted—not just outward, but backward. To another field. Another time.

Sergeant Talbot, who had been promoted to Captain after surviving his first harrowing encounter with Kore.

A soldier long since buried by history, yet never forgotten by her. He had trusted her, not merely as a warrior, but as a guardian—a protector in a world that had already begun to forget what guardians were. That singular act—his faith—became the cornerstone of her identity in this world. It gave shape to her silence, purpose to her permanence, and a name to her otherwise endless wandering.

She sipped bitter coffee, its steam ghosting around her face like the breath of the past, curling and vanishing before her eyes.

Then—

A knock. Sharp. Deliberate. Like the punctuation of fate itself.

She turned.

The door creaked open to reveal a tall figure in Dress Blues—his leatherneck squared away, medals polished to a gleam that seemed almost unnatural under the flickering fluorescent lights. The silver eagle pinned to his chest shone with quiet authority, a silent testament to the rank he carried.

Edith straightened immediately, her spine snapping to rigid attention like a flagpole under strain.

"At ease, Master Guns," the Colonel said with a cool smile that didn't quite reach his eyes.

She relaxed, subtly. Just enough to appear human. Still, the pulse in her neck tightened like a drawn wire.

"Not often we get brass of your caliber, sir," she said evenly, pouring a fresh mug of black coffee without looking away. "Can't imagine the ride was worth it unless someone made one hell of a mistake."

The Colonel didn't take the bait. His expression remained composed, unreadable.

"Well," he said, letting the silence stretch until it nearly snapped, "I came for one person."

Edith's heart skipped—then dropped like a stone into deep water.

"Let me guess... one of the recruits slipped up? What's the charge? Drugs? AWOL?"

The Colonel offered her a patient smile, the kind

that had nothing to do with kindness.

"Fraud."

She set the coffee down slowly, the porcelain rim clicking softly against ceramic. Her voice tightened, but her poise did not.

"I'll cooperate fully, sir. If there's been a misunderstanding about my record, I'll provide all necessary documents."

"Master Gunnery Sergeant..." The Colonel leaned forward slightly, his voice lowering to a level just above a whisper—sharp and precise, a scalpel slipping between ribs. "...cut the shit."

A sharp pause, thick enough to choke on.

"We know exactly what you are," he continued, his tone unchanging, his gaze unrelenting. "The campaigns. The unit logs. The commendations from wars no one even remembers fighting. You're a ghost wrapped in ribbons."

Edith said nothing. Her fingers flexed slightly at her sides—ready, but not nervous. Defensive, yet dignified.

"Colonel... what unit did you say you were with?" she asked, her voice as smooth as a blade drawn across leather.

He grinned then, the way a chess master might when finally tipping his king forward in concession.

From inside his coat, he withdrew a metal

badge—small, unassuming, yet impossibly heavy with implication. He placed it on the desk with a definitive tap that seemed to reverberate through the room.

W.A.S.P.

Worldwide Alien and Superhuman Protocol.

The department no one spoke about outside of dark briefings and classified corridors.

"We watch patterns. Cycles. Anomalies. You're not our first case study… but you're one of the more impressive ones."

His voice softened slightly, tinged with something almost resembling admiration.

"A celestial masquerading as a staff NCO? That takes commitment. I respect that."

He turned toward the door, pausing just long enough for the weight of his words to settle deep into the foundation of the room.

"We'll be watching, Master Gunnery Sergeant Guzman. So don't get any ideas about flying off the grid."

With that, he exited, leaving the door slightly ajar behind him.

Alone now, Edith remained still. Her body didn't flinch, didn't breathe out. But her soul cracked at the edges, fine fractures splintering outward like ice underfoot. Her mind reeled—calculating threats, escape options, allies still hidden. The past was catching up, boots in the dirt, orders in the wind.

And she had just been activated.

* * *

Edith dropped from the sky like a dying star, her boots crashing into scorched soil that sizzled underfoot. The impact sent small clouds of ash and ember spiraling into the air. The atmosphere was thick with the choking scent of burning earth—coiling smoke trailing like ghostly fingers through a sky painted with blood-orange light.

The forest before her was no longer a place of life, but a graveyard. The trees were nothing more than blackened skeletons, clawing at the heavens in silent agony. What once thrived here had been unearthed—defiled—by something ancient and furious.

Her breath hitched.

Not from exertion, but from dread.

She stepped forward slowly, her once-commanding gait now stilted by a heaviness she could not shake. The soles of her boots crunched over cinders and bone-splintered branches, each footfall louder than it should have been in the unnatural hush that blanketed the world.

Before her loomed what remained of the tree—

the ancient prison.

It had once pulsed with divine light, a testament to sacrifice, its very fibers threaded with the guilt and hopes of centuries. Guarded by blood and oath. Now it was nothing but broken, burning timber, strewn like battlefield wreckage across the smoldering landscape. The roots—once sacred, once alive—were now exposed veins of charcoal, still twitching in the dying embers as if mourning their failure.

Edith fell to one knee, her posture collapsing under the weight of realization.

Her fingers sifted through the smoking soil, touching the fractured remains of the binding wards. Shattered glyphs glimmered faintly beneath her touch, their arcane energy bleeding out into the earth like the last gasps of a dying heartbeat.

She whispered, "No…" Her voice cracked, dry as parchment and heavy with despair.

She didn't need confirmation. She could feel it—like static crawling beneath her skin, like a scream echoing in the very marrow of her bones. Something had breached the seal. Something with power. Something with purpose.

Her sister.

Kore had been released.

Or worse—had awakened.

Edith's heart thundered against her ribs as she

scanned the treeline, her senses flaring to their fullest extent. The stench of sulfur laced the air, mingling with the smoldering scent of ancient wood and something metallic—something sharp and predatory.

"This wasn't time," she muttered under her breath, her eyes narrowing with grim clarity. "Someone pulled her out."

The realization struck her like a blade driven deep into her gut.

Someone wanted this.

This wasn't chaos. It was orchestration.

A deliberate act designed to undo the one thing she had spent lifetimes trying to preserve: containment.

The forest around her groaned and shifted, as if waking from a nightmare too terrible to name. Distant, low rumbles rolled through the valley—thunder with teeth and breath.

Edith rose slowly, her stance shifting, her body drawing strength from the fear that refused to leave her. Her eyes, fierce now, glowed faintly beneath the shifting shadows of the smoke and flame. Her fear did not abandon her—but it calcified into something harder. Something that could fight.

"I warned you, Kore," she whispered to the wind, her voice steel-edged. "If you ever broke free again, I would not hesitate."

But even as she spoke, doubt laced the words like poison.

Because she wasn't sure anymore. Not after everything. Not after all she had lost.

And somewhere—beyond the veil of trees, beyond the curtain of smoke and flame—

Kore smiled.

* * *

Forty-Eight Hours Earlier

The forest breathes unnaturally.

Its trees groan with old, secret weight. A low mist creeps along the moss-choked roots, clinging to the feet of soldiers like tendrils desperate for warmth. The tree—the tree—glows with a pulse that isn't light, but memory. It beats slowly, sickly, like a god's dying heartbeat.

A gloved hand brushes against its bark.

"Why the hell is it glowing like that?" asks one of the agents, his voice hushed, reverent, disturbed.

"We found what we came for," replies Agent Miranda Baker, her voice unshaken. Her tactical suit is matte black, reinforced carbon weave, glowing faintly with linked telemetry and biofeedback

234

nodes. Across her vest—bold and ghost-white—
four unmistakable letters: W.A.S.P.

Her team fans out, securing the perimeter with
sharp, practiced movements. Their boots crunch
over the leaves, snapping twigs and debris like
brittle bones. Drones hum overhead, mapping
the strange terrain, scanning for heat signatures
or movement—finding nothing but cold whispers
stitched into the air.

Miranda lowers a strange optic helmet over her
face—its lens clicking with mechanized precision.
Through it, the forest shifts: spectral overlays, heat
ghosts, and pulse trails bloom across her vision.
She adjusts the calibrator embedded in her grip.

"Montanez, staff."

A slender tech hands her a long, metallic rod
lined with small, rune-etched bulbs. She slams it
into the earth with a brutal precision.

The ground screams.

Light pours from the point of impact—golden
smoke billows upward, glowing like holy fire, but
tainted with something darker. Something off.
The dirt cracks. The forest shakes. A long stone
stairwell unravels from beneath the roots, spiraling
into darkness like a wound torn open in the world's
flesh.

"Move!" she commands, descending into the
subterranean crypt. "Eyes sharp. No engagement

unless I give the call."

The air down here is thick with damp rot and buried power. Glowing sigils burn along the walls—runes that seem to slither when stared at too long. Par-script. A language older than the dirt they walk upon. The light dims the deeper they descend, until they reach it—

A cocoon of light.

Massive. Pulsing.

Suspended from the cavern ceiling by strands of energy like angelic silk soaked in molten sunfire. It radiates heat. Hunger. Something stirs within.

"What the hell is that?" whispers SPC Keller, raising his weapon reflexively.

"Thermals confirm—something's inside," Miranda says, her voice steady, but her muscles coil tight with anticipation.

Above ground, the tension shatters.

Agent Lock spins—rifle up—his pupils blown wide with terror.

"I heard something," he breathes. "Something's talking to me."

"You're compromised. Put the weapon down," warns another soldier, already training his aim with rigid hands.

But it's too late.

The whisper returns—not sound, but vibration. It skitters through the base of Lock's skull like a thousand insect legs, rewriting thought with dread. His hands tremble. His breath quickens. His trigger finger tightens.

"I… I can't stop it," he whimpers.

Below, Miranda's hand inches toward the cocoon. Her glove grazes the radiant surface—

A shockwave detonates from above.

The cave shrieks. Earth trembles, raining dust and loose stone. The cocoon shudders violently, threads of energy unraveling in fits of light.

The cocoon bursts in a storm of divine energy, and something reaches through—a hand, crimson and veined with black, seizing Miranda's wrist with impossible strength.

"What the—"

The light collapses inward, vanishing into a singularity of heat and silence.

And from that devoured brilliance, something rises.

A woman—and not.

Kore.

Her form blossoms from the void like a nightmare made flesh. Her skin ripples with hues of red like molten silk, her hair wet-black and clinging to her sharpened features. Jagged horns curl upward from her forehead like the crown of an executioner. Black wings snap open with an audible crack, like ancient bones broken and reborn.

She floats, levitating effortlessly, lifting Miranda like a child's doll.

"Fire! Shoot it!" Miranda screams, voice cracking with desperation.

The agents unleash hell. Rifles stutter. Muzzle flashes paint the cavern walls in fits of orange and white.

But Kore does not flinch.

She watches.

And with a single, fluid sweep of her wings, she casts the bullets aside like dust caught in a hurricane. Then she moves—faster than sight, a blur of wrath and beauty.

She tears through the squad with animal elegance—limbs ripped free in bursts of gore, torsos flung against stone with bone-snapping force. Their screams echo once, sharp and brutal—then fade to silence. Blood mists the cave, drifting in a slow, crimson haze.

Only Miranda remains.

She stumbles backward, pistol trembling in her grasp, staring up at the hovering monstrosity with wide, disbelieving eyes.

"What the hell are you?" she whispers, her voice almost stolen by fear.

Kore tilts her head slowly, her eyes glowing like burning rubies framed in a maelstrom of shadow.

Her voice drips from her lips—silk soaked in

brimstone.

"I am free."

12

W.A.S.P.

E dith staggered through the ruptured cavern mouth, her boots grinding over broken shale and crumbling stone. The darkness inside welcomed her like a tomb, swallowing what little light remained behind her. Her breath hitched as she descended into the cavern's belly, where the damp air reeked of scorched ozone, copper, and death.

This had once been a sanctum—a hallowed retreat hidden from the eyes of men and monsters alike. A sacred refuge carved from the living rock, guarded by spells so old even the stars had forgotten them. But now...

Now, it was a slaughterhouse.

Her boots slipped slightly as she stepped forward, and that was when she saw it: bodies strewn like discarded puppets, shredded beyond recognition.

Flesh peeled from bone, viscera flung across the cave walls in abstract bursts of horror. The corpses hung in various stages of ruin, some embedded into the jagged stone like grotesque ornaments. Blood pooled at her feet, thick and sticky, seeping into the fractured earth and crackling beneath magical residue that shimmered with a dying, sickly glow.

A gory greenhouse of chaos.

Edith clutched her gut as the bile rose hot and fast in her throat. She had seen war. She had seen genocide. She had witnessed the cruelty of fallen angels and the cold indifference of ancient gods. But this—this was something else. This was surgical carnage masked in primal fury, a desecration that screamed of rage barely restrained.

The remnants of W.A.S.P. tacticians littered the cavern floor, their high-grade gear torn open like discarded wrapping paper, their faces frozen in grotesque masks of unholy terror. These weren't mere soldiers. These were elite. Hardened. Trained. And they hadn't stood a chance.

She turned her gaze to the fractured remnants of the pod—the prison that had once held her sister, bound beneath layers of woven light and ancient seals. Now, only scorched sigils and flickering traces of broken wards remained. The divine lock, once impossibly strong, had been ruptured by arrogance or ignorance... or both.

Her knees buckled, and she collapsed into a crouch, hands trembling against the blood-slicked stone. Someone had found Kore. Someone had blown the whistle. Someone had pulled apart the very chains that held back the end of days.

The cold truth slithered into her gut like a living thing: she had no idea where her sister had gone. No leads. No divine whispers. No prophetic dreams. Only a world of chaos waiting, eager for a queen of carnage to rise.

Edith stumbled out of the ruined cavern, her face pale beneath streaks of dirt, blood, and ash. The once-hidden region—nestled beyond the reach of satellites, sorcery, or surveillance—now felt like an open wound. The skies above, once her cloak and comfort, now stretched wide and empty like a mouth preparing to scream.

"Dammit," she whispered, her voice raw against the heavy air, eyes scanning the twisted treetops, searching for something—anything—that could tell her where Kore had fled. "I should've buried her deeper."

There was no time left for mourning. No time left for regret. Only pursuit.

The Halphobs were gone. She hadn't seen them in what felt like eons. Perhaps they had done the only sensible thing—isolated themselves at the frayed edges of reality, beyond the reach of men, monsters, and even gods. Edith had no way of reaching them now, no allies to call upon, no hidden doors left to pry open.

She needed answers. And she needed them now.

One name buzzed in her head like a dying signal on a shortwave radio.

Colonel Humphrey.

She remembered the insignia on the card he had left—a black sigil, sharp and unmistakable. The same logo stitched into the gear now drenched in blood and entrails at her feet. Four letters, burned into her mind like a brand:

W.A.S.P.

They knew who she was. Knew what she was.

And they still came.

Edith narrowed her eyes toward the bleeding horizon, her fists clenching and unclenching at her sides. Her wings remained hidden beneath the mortal skin she wore, but the divine ache behind her shoulder blades screamed for release, for vengeance, for reckoning.

And she promised herself one thing:

She would find them.

And she would make them answer.

Edith shoved open the door to her battalion office, her boots slamming against the linoleum like thunder rolling through concrete. The lights above buzzed faintly, casting a flickering haze across the dim room. She gripped a blackened W.A.S.P. badge in one hand, her other clutching a cell phone mid-dial—ready to call someone, anyone who might explain the bloodbath she had just witnessed in that forest.

But then she stopped.

Colonel Humphrey sat in her chair, perfectly still, bathed in the cold light spilling through the blinds. His fingers were steepled. His polished boots crossed at the ankle. Calm. Too calm.

"Looking for someone?" he asked, his voice carrying an oily, bureaucratic ease—like a snake coiled beneath velvet.

Edith slammed the badge down on the desk between them. "What did you do?" she snapped, her breath ragged, fury barely restrained. Her hands trembled—not from fear, but from the pressure of holding back everything inside her.

The Colonel didn't flinch. He simply raised a brow.

"Easy, Master Gunnery Sergeant. I still wear the bird," he said coolly, motioning to the silver eagle gleaming on his collar.

"You have no idea what you've just unleashed."

"Oh, I think I do," he said, leaning back in her chair, fingers tapping together with a metronomic patience. "You've got a sibling on the loose. I've got a missing operative. Looks like we both have family issues."

"You had no business poking around that cave."

"And yet, we found quite the Pandora's box, didn't we?" His tone never rose, but each word slithered like a scalpel carving into soft flesh. "We monitor anomalies. Beings like you who slip through the cracks. A few months back, a prisoner was hit by lightning—his body mutated by something not of this Earth. That was our wake-up call. You were the siren after."

Edith's fists clenched until her knuckles whitened. "You violated sovereignty. You desecrated a prison you didn't understand."

"And you," he interrupted sharply, "violated federal code by falsifying your identity, concealing your physiology, and endangering every life you've come into contact with."

"You sent children into a minefield."

"I sent trained tacticians," he shot back, his voice as sharp as broken glass. "And your sister turned them into ribbons."

Edith's face hardened, her jaw locking. "You think this is over?"

The Colonel's phone rang. He picked it up without breaking eye contact.

"Humphrey," he answered crisply. A pause. "Baker? Good to hear your voice. Medical's waiting. Debrief after triage."

He ended the call and slowly returned the handset to its cradle with a faint, deliberate click.

"Well," he said, almost cheerfully, "looks like my problem just walked out of the woods."

"What?" Edith growled, stepping closer.

"My operative survived."

"No," she whispered, her voice thin and disbelieving. Her eyes widened with dread. "Kore doesn't show mercy. She doesn't leave survivors."

"Maybe this time she did."

"That's not mercy," Edith said, her voice cracking like brittle glass. "That's a warning."

The Colonel stood, brushing invisible lint from his chest. His ribbons and medals clinked softly with the movement, a metallic echo of silent authority.

"You want to stay here?" he said. "Then handle your bloodline. You have ninety-six hours to find your sister and put her back in whatever cage you pulled her from."

Edith stepped forward, her voice low and trembling with fury. "You don't know what you're asking. The seal that held her was powered by a species that no longer exists. The only one who could draw the mutagen from her is dead. She's stronger now than she's ever been."

"Then I guess you'd better get creative," the

Colonel replied coldly, his eyes hard and unyielding.

"This is your mess," she spat. "You and your damn agency lit the fuse."

"No," he said, his gaze sharpening. "You brought the bomb. We just tripped over the timer."

She seethed, her chest rising and falling with barely contained rage.

"I do this on my terms," she said through gritted teeth.

"Good," he replied, flashing a mirthless smile. "Just be quick about it. Or W.A.S.P. will clean up the mess for you. And when we do? You're on the next transport back to wherever you came from."

He started for the door, his boots echoing across the floor, then paused, casting one final look over his shoulder with a condescending grin.

"I'd get a move on if I were you. Tick-tock, Master Gunnery Sergeant."

The door clicked shut behind him, and Edith stood frozen in the silence, her mind spiraling with dread. The clock was ticking. Her sister was free. And the world had no idea what horror was about to walk its streets.

* * *

Miranda's breath came shallow, trembling in the

flickering dark. Her boots scraped weakly against the blood-slicked floor of the W.A.S.P. headquarters' ruined laboratory. She stood suspended by a coarse rope wound tight beneath her chin, her arms wrenched behind her back, wrists bruised and bloodied. The rope creaked above her—a grim metronome to the silence of death that surrounded her.

Around her, the lab was a butcher's gallery.

Bodies dangled over shattered equipment, torsos split open like ruptured pods, limbs twisted at wrong angles, their faces locked in expressions of final terror. Walls were smeared with arterial arcs, as if painted by some deranged artist mid-mania. The glow of ruined monitors cast a cold blue light across the carnage, flickering weakly like dying stars.

"If you're going to kill me," Miranda spat, chin twitching toward the unseen presence in the dark, "just get it over with."

A sound. Soft. Like silk whispering across old bone.

And then she saw them—two burning embers suspended in the black. Eyes. Watching her.

Kore stepped into the ruin like a goddess risen from rot.

Her crimson skin shimmered in the shadows like polished bloodstone. Her black wings curled upward like claws reaching to drag the sky down. And yet it was her voice—*modern, sharpened, learned*—that chilled Miranda deeper than any nightmare.

"This is how they held me," Kore said softly. "Bound like a dog. Stretched between bone and breath. I was to be slaughtered like cattle. Like something lesser."

"You definitely seem like one," Miranda said, eyes locked with Kore's. "Animals kill when they're hungry."

Kore's smile split slowly. "And who says I'm not?"

She hovered closer, boots never touching the gore-slicked ground. Her gaze flicked across the hanging corpses like they were relics of a lesser age—curiosities, not crimes.

"I've studied the evolution of this world while I slept. Your cultures, your weapons, your language, your... *trends*." She tilted her head. "But the one constant across millennia? You always fear what you don't understand."

Kore leaned in, face inches from Miranda's, her voice a velvet noose.

"And then you kill it."

"You're doing the same," Miranda said through clenched teeth. "You don't understand us. So you butcher us. Not as vengeance—*as fear*."

Kore blinked, and for a moment, Miranda

thought she saw… amusement.

"Profiling me, Agent?" Kore purred. "Cute. You read minds in a cubicle. I read the marrow of worlds."

"You're full of shit," Miranda snapped. "You hacked our systems. That's all. You're not divine. Just another thief with a God complex."

Kore laughed—low, soft, like the shiver of metal against skin.

"Thief? No. I do not take. I *earn*. I endured torment beneath stone temples. Fought creatures older than language. *Survived Par*. I've never stolen a thing. Not even the lives I've ended."

"You've stolen *thousands*," Miranda said. "Millions, maybe."

Kore's eyes narrowed. "And now… I wish to *create*."

Miranda's face twisted in confusion. "What?"

"There's something in this realm. Something your agency cannot explain. I sought its records, but even your archives are blind to it."

She floated closer again. "You've been tracking it, haven't you?"

Miranda stared at her. "Wait… are you trying to *breed* with it?"

Kore didn't blink. Her voice dropped to a deep, guttural rumble.

"I am *royalty*," she hissed, "a queen cast down

by blood and by betrayal. My father damned my skin. My sister sealed me in light. I pity your children, for they are born into corruption and silenced by institutions. But my child… *my child* shall be something new."

"You're a lunatic."

Kore leaned closer, her breath hot against Miranda's face. "Where. Is. It."

"You really think I'm scared of rope and threats?" Miranda said, her voice steady now, cold and clear. "You can hang me from the rafters—but I'll die before I give you *anything*."

"The rope," Kore whispered, "is not your punishment."

She raised her clawed hand to Miranda's temple. "It's just… an introduction."

The moment her fingers touched skin, the agony was *instant*. It wasn't physical pain. It was something deeper. Something buried. Miranda gasped as searing energy flooded her skull, splitting her thoughts like rotten fruit. *Visions* crashed through her mind—children burning, the sky bleeding, entire cities dragged into a blackened sea. The screams weren't from others—they were *hers*, drawn from her own veins like poison.

Her limbs shook. Her mouth opened in a silent howl.

And Kore drank it in. Not with satisfaction, but

with stillness. She fed not on fear—but understanding.

"I know you now," Kore said softly. "Every regret. Every betrayal. Every lie you told yourself to keep breathing. You think you're strong because you endured."

She leaned close, her lips to Miranda's ear.

"But you are *not like me.*"

Then, without warning, Kore released her.

Miranda collapsed to the floor, gasping like a drowning woman. The rope around her neck lay loose. The pain receded like a retreating tide—but what it left behind was worse. *She felt hollow.*

"I'll come for your creature soon," Kore said, turning toward the dark corridor. "And when I do, I won't be alone."

She vanished into shadow—leaving only blood, broken lights, and the dying hum of a world beginning to crack.

13

Cataclysmic

The ticking clock in Edith's soul roared louder than any drill cadence echoing through the battalion. Her deadline loomed like an executioner's blade—ninety-six hours to bring down her sister or be exiled from the very world she had bled to protect. And the truth was… W.A.S.P. wouldn't wait that long.

Exiting her office with urgency masked behind tight discipline, Edith moved through the corridor like a shadow with weight. Her boots struck tile like a slow war drum. As she passed the comms lounge, a group of junior Marines huddled around a mounted television, their rapt gazes glued to a breaking news bulletin.

The screen pulsed with static and fire. A trembling reporter stood outside a scorched compound—his face pale, his voice brittle.

"We're receiving reports of a catastrophic attack on a secure facility linked to U.S. intelligence. Over two hundred operatives confirmed dead. Unverified footage reveals blood-red skies over the blast site... officials claim the nature of the attack may be—*anomalous.*"

Behind the reporter, an aerial image flickered— brief, grainy, but unmistakable.

Four letters burned through smoke and ruin: W.A.S.P.

Edith's blood ran cold.

Her sister hadn't waited. Kore had already carved a path of ruin straight through W.A.S.P.'s stronghold—and they hadn't even known what they were holding.

"Where is this?" Edith asked, voice flat, eyes locked to the screen.

A young Marine, Lance Corporal Hayes, looked up, startled by the tone.

"Charith, Master Guns. Some town out near Vegas," he said, straightening instinctively under her gaze. "You think we're gonna be sent in?"

His voice carried that reckless spark only youth can afford—an edge of excitement, the kind that hadn't yet tasted real horror.

Edith didn't answer right away. Her thoughts roared with images: a sister reborn in rage... clouds bled crimson... cities turned into graves.

"They'll send the Guard," she said, tight-lipped. "Lighten up, Devil Dog."

But deep in her chest, her heart pounded like the knell of a coming storm. No Guard unit would stop this. No airstrike. No perimeter. No drone. This wasn't war. This was myth. A nightmare that W.A.S.P. had unwittingly unleashed upon a fragile world.

And yet, no one knew it but her.

Edith clenched the W.A.S.P. access card in her palm until its edges bit into her skin. Her identity wouldn't stay hidden much longer. They'd dig up the truth. They'd uncover her history, her false records, the lies of a woman who had existed for centuries, not decades. There was no running anymore.

And in that quiet clarity…

She rose.

"It's gotta be me," she whispered, almost to herself.

The Marines turned, confused.

"Master Guns?"

Edith looked around. The flickering light from the television painted her face in hues of blue and flame. She could hear it again—the tremor in her blood, the pulse of her realm calling her to act. Not as Edith. Not as Master Gunnery Sergeant. But as Ara.

"Stand clear," she said.

Before they could react, her body arched. Her breath caught—and then came the sound: a sharp, divine *tear* of air and fabric as her wings burst forth, golden and immense, unfurling with thunderous might. Her desert cammies shredded like paper beneath the emergence. Feathers—not of flesh, but of celestial flame—fanned across the air like war banners made of starlight.

The squad froze. No words. Just awe.

Her golden aura ignited, crawling across her skin in radiant pulses. Her face shimmered with power long suppressed. Her once-muted features now glowed with the full majesty of Par royalty—golden hair cascading like sunlight, her eyes alight with divine determination.

They stared as if witnessing the rise of a god.

Edith stepped forward, the marble silence of the room cracking under her footfalls. No orders. No fanfare. Just presence. She crossed the threshold of the battalion office and emerged onto the drill field, the midday sun paling against her radiance.

A gust of wind rolled across the base.

And then—she flew.

With a single beat of her wings, the Earth dropped away beneath her. Dust kicked across the field. Hats flew. Junior Marines stumbled back in disbelief, their jaws open, unable to comprehend what they'd seen.

"What the hell was that?" one whispered.

But she was already gone—a golden comet streaking through the sky, tearing toward the blood-red stormclouds gathering over Charith.

The final war had begun.

And she would not run from it.

* * *

The sky above the W.A.S.P. compound had turned into a wound.

Crimson clouds churned overhead, swollen with rage and ash, as if the heavens themselves were hemorrhaging. The facility below, once a symbol of impenetrable authority, now lay silent and blackened, a graveyard for secrets. What the news cameras had captured earlier was only the beginning. What remained now was a sterilized silence, broken only by the low hiss of still-smoldering debris and the faint hum of exposed conduits in the wind.

Edith descended from the sky like a judgment— her golden wings carving through the storm-laced air, her eyes scanning the carnage below with the weight of centuries behind them. She touched down lightly on scorched pavement, combat boots landing amid puddles of blood and twisted rebar.

Her golden aura flickered against the dead steel and melted glass of the facility's perimeter.

This was not justice. This was retribution masquerading as grief.

She approached the sealed hangar, her hand rising as radiant energy coiled around her palm. But before she could release the blast—

The doors shuddered. A groaning metallic screech echoed as the hangar slowly parted, exhaling darkness into the daylight. A long corridor stretched ahead—lit faintly by flickering emergency strips and framed by twisted remains of high-tech hardware. It felt like entering a mechanical crypt.

Edith stepped inside.

"Kore!" she called, her voice ringing sharp as a blade across the steel. "I know you hear me!"

Silence answered—then a faint *clang* echoed through the distant dark, too intentional to be debris. Edith's wings tightened slightly against her back.

"I know you hate me. You *should*. But I did what I had to. I saved the world from your pain." Her voice cracked, her eyes narrowed. "And I'll do it again, if I must."

Another clang—closer now. But there was no response.

"Come out," Edith whispered, not pleading but

demanding, "and we can end this together. We don't need to keep bleeding this world dry."

Suddenly, a figure stumbled from the far corridor, disoriented and limping. It was a woman—her face cut, her tactical gear shredded, and blood dripping down her arm in thick rivulets.

"Help me…" the voice rasped. "Please…"

Edith's stance shifted. Her hand flexed cautiously.

"Who are you?" she asked, her tone clipped. "Speak clearly."

"You're one of them," the woman murmured. "Like *her*. Aren't you?"

She collapsed to her knees. Edith approached slowly.

"Where is she?" Edith demanded. "Don't waste my time."

"She… she tore through everything," the woman gasped, clutching her ribs. "Killed my whole squad. I don't know how I made it out alive. I've been hiding."

"And yet," Edith said, eyes narrowing, "she spared *you*."

The woman flinched, just slightly.

"There's no time for this," she snapped. "The generator's down. If we don't reboot comms, reinforcements won't know what's happening. We need to act *now*."

"You expect me to believe that after what I've seen?" Edith's voice sharpened. "Why not call for help before?"

"I *couldn't!*" the woman barked. "The system's fried—look, I can walk you through the override protocol. Just help me get to the control room!"

Edith hesitated. Her instincts warred with logic. Then—

"Bethany's going to destroy everything."

The name slipped from the woman's lips like venom.

And Edith froze.

Something snapped in her gut.

"What... did you say?"

"Bethany," the woman repeated, breath trembling. "That's its name, isn't it?"

Silence.

Stillness.

Like the breath before a scream.

Edith turned her head slightly, her gaze sharp as daggers.

"No one knows that name," she said, slowly. "Not unless they've lived it."

Her eyes locked onto the woman's.

"Where did you hear that?"

The woman stammered—too late. Edith's hand shot out, catching a sudden swing of a haymaker mid-air. Her grip locked like iron.

Then it changed.

The woman's flesh melted like candle wax in her grasp—peeling into a crimson sheen. Black veins pulsed through her neck, and her nails curled into hooked talons. Horns coiled from her skull, and her hair bled into a matted, night-black tangle.

Kore.

Her lips curled into a smirk, her eyes twin infernos.

"So close," she hissed, "and yet thou still thinkest thyself the clever one."

Edith didn't flinch. Not this time.

"You always were a terrible liar," she said coldly. "But a damn good actress."

Kore snarled, her hand burning with demonic energy.

"You imprisoned me! You stripped me of power. Of identity. Of *vengeance!*"

"And you burned your chance at forgiveness," Edith growled, her wings flaring behind her. "This ends here, sister. No more speeches. No more tricks."

The corridor trembled with the weight of their clash yet to come.

And in that moment, nothing else existed but sister against sister, blood against blood, war against the last chance at redemption.

14

A Broken Promise

PAR

The corridor is carved from despair—stone walls soaked in mildew, blood, and centuries of sorrow. The deeper Ara walks, the heavier the air becomes, thick with grief and the metallic scent of rusted chains. Her glowing palms barely light the path ahead, casting ghostly reflections on the damp stone. The Kelxsiar prison lies far beneath Par's forgotten spires, and here—buried beneath its cruelty—is her sister.

Kore.

Ara stops at the cell.

Behind the bars, slumped against the corner like a broken doll, is Kore. Her skin is crimson and cracked, veins webbed black like poison beneath parchment. Her claws twitch occasionally, an unconscious reminder of the pain that never truly leaves. Her wings—tattered, useless—hang behind her like withered shadows, drooping low to the filthy ground. Her eyes are open but unfocused, gleaming dimly with tears that refuse to fall.

She doesn't look up.

"Kore," Ara whispers, kneeling against the cold iron. "I found you."

Kore shifts slightly. Her voice is hoarse, brittle from silence and suffering.

"Don't say my name like it matters."

"It does matter. You matter."

"Not to him," Kore rasps. "Not to Par. Not to anyone but the guards who feed on my pain."

Ara slips her trembling hands between the bars, reaching toward her sister's broken face. The metal bites into her skin, but she doesn't care.

"To me. Always to me."

She wipes away the black-streaked tears, fingers shaking from a storm of emotion. The contact stings—like fire and frost meeting—but Ara doesn't flinch. She holds on, refusing to pull away.

"I was just a child," Kore says, her voice splintering with raw hurt. "They said I was cursed. Mutated. Wrong. Father called me an infection… He let them put me down here like I was less. Like

I was never even his daughter."

Ara's voice cracks, her heart shattering inside her chest.

"He was afraid of what he didn't understand. But I'm not afraid of you. I will never be afraid of you. And I'll never leave you here."

Kore's dull eyes shift, locking onto Ara's face with a slow, painful effort. They burn—not with anger—but with something infinitely more fragile.

Hope.

"You say that," she murmurs, voice hollow, "but this place… this place is where people vanish."

"Then let me show you where I see us," Ara says, voice trembling with conviction.

She places her glowing fingers gently on Kore's temples. The red-skinned girl flinches at the touch—then, gradually, stills under her sister's warmth.

Both sisters close their eyes.

And suddenly, the stone walls dissolve.

Kore's mind opens—and she sees it.

A golden garden, untouched by death. A sky alight with shimmering stars, swirling in brilliant constellations. Trees that breathe with living energy, their leaves singing with the hum of existence. Rivers of light weaving between vast, welcoming mountains like veins of peace. Laughter rides the breeze, and warmth blooms in every corner of the endless horizon. A realm not built for conquest or torment—but for healing. For life.

Kore gasps, a sharp, broken sound. Her breath catches in her throat like a sob too heavy to release.

"What is this?" she whispers, her voice no longer brittle but trembling with awe.

"It's real," Ara says fiercely, her hands steady against Kore's skin. "I saw it in a vision. And I believe it's waiting for us. Together."

Kore shudders, tears welling up again—this time from something she cannot name, cannot fight.

"No... no, Ara. This is a dream. Just a dream. I'll never see this. Not someone like me."

"You will," Ara says, her voice fierce and breaking all at once. "We will. I swear it."

Bootsteps echo down the corridor—harsh, heavy—the Kelxsiar guards, closing in.

Ara jolts upright, panic slicing through her chest like a knife.

"They'll catch you—go!" Kore cries out, her voice cracking with urgency.

"I can't leave you again—" Ara pleads, torn between terror and loyalty.

"You have to!" Kore shouts, louder now. "Don't make me watch you rot too!"

Ara backs away, hands still aglow, tears streaming freely down her face. Every step feels like betrayal, like ripping her own heart in half.

"I'll come back," she promises, voice hoarse with grief. "I swear to the stars, I will get you out of here."

"Don't promise what you can't keep," Kore whispers, her voice already fading like smoke.

"I promise," Ara says again, her voice steel wrapped in sorrow—and sprints into the darkness.

Kore is left alone.

The guards do not come to her cell. They do not speak. They move past, their steps a distant thunder.

And Kore's eyes stay closed.

Because in that flicker of shared light, she saw it.

For the first time in her life…

She saw something worth believing in.

15

Freedom

The sky bled crimson.

From cities to deserts, oceans to tundras, the world tilted their heads toward the heavens— not in awe, but in dread. Above them, two celestial titans—sisters by blood, enemies by fate—tore the very fabric of the firmament.

Golden brilliance collided with infernal red, and every strike cracked the heavens like the wrath of gods. Sonic shockwaves rippled outward in concentric agony, shaking glass, rattling bones, and warping the clouds themselves. It was not a battle— it was a reckoning.

Edith's radiant form blazed like a dying star, every movement an aria of controlled fury. Her wings cut the sky like scythes of judgment, trailing gold in streaks that stitched heaven back together just as it fell apart. Across from her, Kore hovered in a storm of burning red light, her body twisted by rage and rejection. Her once-sorrowful eyes now burned with voidfire—pure, vengeful energy that pulsed like a heartbeat about to burst.

They moved as one, two gods locked in a rhythm of war. Fists struck like meteors. Bodies whipped across the horizon, leaving sonic scars in their wake.

The Earth beneath them held its breath.

Kore roared, swirling red energy into her palms. It wasn't power—it was loathing made flesh. Her aura flared, cracking the air as she hurled it forward with a scream that splintered sound itself.

Edith didn't answer with a beam of her own. She *moved*—a sudden, breathtaking pivot through the air. Her body somersaulted above the blast, letting it tear through clouds and sky as she dove. She flipped mid-air, light gleaming off her golden skin, and struck Kore with a flurry of savage kicks. Each impact sent shockwaves through the air, knocking the red-skinned sister off-kilter.

Edith coiled behind her like a serpent of light and locked Kore in a brutal chokehold.

"Don't make me kill you!" Edith growled through clenched teeth. "None of this will give you what you want. You're killing the *wrong people!*"

"You don't *know* what I want!" Kore snarled, her voice choked with more than air—betrayal, grief, abandonment.

"I do. I *do.* I've seen it. I've shown you what we could have. Peace, Kore. Freedom. Together."

"You *promised* me that paradise," Kore hissed, rage twisting her lips. "And then you *locked me away.* You broke it."

With a savage twist, Kore hooked her foot behind Edith's leg and yanked. The golden warrior lost balance, tumbling mid-air—only for Kore to follow up with three blinding strikes to the face, each one cracking against her skull like war drums.

And then came the claws.

Inky black talons erupted from Kore's fingers. She slammed them into Edith's neck, lifting her like a broken doll. With a guttural snarl, she hurled her sister downward.

Edith's body tore through the air, spinning, bleeding light. The Earth rushed up to meet her like a waiting executioner.

But she caught herself.

She flipped, braked hard with a burst of divine wind, and launched back upward like a meteor in reverse. Golden wings shattered the sound barrier as she closed the distance and caught Kore by her corrupted wing, twisting with brutal torque.

"Enough!" Edith screamed, spinning and hurling Kore across the atmosphere.

Kore spiraled, dazed—until a searing blast of

golden light slammed into her face, cutting her flight short with explosive finality. Her body flipped end over end, limp in the sky.

Edith didn't wait.

She flew like judgment incarnate, caught Kore mid-fall, and *drove* her downward—through clouds, through air, through heaven's last mercy. The impact shook the world.

A crater split open below.

The ground cracked like brittle bone beneath the force. Shockwaves fanned out, flattening the landscape for miles. Dust and debris rained down like ashes from a celestial funeral pyre.

* * *

Kore lay shattered in the wreckage of her wrath— her crimson flesh torn, her obsidian blood pooling thick beneath her like oil from a ruptured god. Her wings, once dreadful in their majesty, now hung limp and twitching—spasming shadows, broken and glistening with gore. Her breathing came in rattled gulps, hitching through clenched teeth as her body pulsed with fractured rage.

From above, Edith descended—her golden form marred and dim, a flickering halo of exhausted light trailing behind her. The wind around her shifted uneasily, as if the air itself feared what must come next.

She landed silently, the earth cracking beneath her feet.

With grim purpose, she stepped forward and gripped Kore's matted hair—slick with sweat and blood—and yanked her head back. The motion peeled a grunt from Kore's lungs, her eyes fluttering open with glassy defiance. Her throat was bared, neck arched in bitter offering.

A blade of light bloomed in Edith's palm—a weapon forged from pure celestial fire, humming with judgment. She brought it to Kore's throat, the heat of it singing the flesh just above her pulse.

"You lied," Kore rasped, her voice fraying like unraveling silk. "You promised me freedom. You said you saw me. And in the end, you treated me like the rest. Like a thing. A monster."

Edith's jaw clenched.

"No, Kore," she said, her voice a low tremor. "You did this. You *chose* to become what they feared. You chose to be merciless. You let the hatred rot you from the inside out. You're not a monster because of what you are. You're a monster because you *wanted* to be."

Kore coughed, her mouth curling into something between a sneer and a smirk. "Then do it. Do what everyone else has always wanted to do. Finish me."

Edith pressed the blade to her throat. The light

hissed as it kissed blood. Her hand trembled, just enough to betray her resolve.

She could feel the clock ticking—W.A.S.P. would come. They would *end* Kore if she didn't. They'd end *both* of them if they had to.

But her heart… her cursed, aching heart…

She couldn't do it.

The blade dissolved, dimming to a harmless shimmer. Her hands dropped.

Kore's eyes lit up with infernal revelation.

"Stupid bitch," she snarled.

Without warning, Kore's wing lashed out—hard, sharp, and venomous. It impaled Edith clean through the shoulder, like a spear forged in hell. A second wing followed, piercing her opposite shoulder with surgical violence.

Edith screamed, golden ichor spurting from her wounds. Her limbs went slack as the wings lifted her off the ground—dangling her like a holy effigy hoisted in blasphemy.

Kore floated to meet her, their faces inches apart, her breath like brimstone. Her body began to pulse—veins black as space creeping along her arms, crawling like parasites toward Edith's face.

"Let me show you what I see," Kore whispered.

The tendrils of corruption snaked into Edith's temples. Her golden eyes flickered—and then turned red.

A vision exploded behind them: A world devoured by fire. A scorched planet where oceans boiled, skies bled ash, and forests screamed as they burned. Upon a throne of bone and scorched earth stood Kore—unrecognizable, fully mutated, her body an abomination of horns, talons, and nightmare wings. And in her arms... a child. Swaddled in cloth, cooing innocently—while its mother, this *thing*, smiled down upon it with a predator's pride.

Edith tore her gaze away, gasping—but Kore wasn't done.

Flames erupted around them, crackling with otherworldly heat. With a sickening rip, Kore wrenched her wings from Edith's flesh, sending the golden warrior plummeting like a shot angel.

She crashed into the ground, a crater blooming around her broken form.

But the tendrils remained.

They coiled, black and slick, around her limbs—snapping tight. The air howled as the tendrils hardened into *chains*, searing with molten red sigils. They tightened with every breath Edith took, constricting, squeezing, crushing.

Edith screamed, her voice cracking open the silence like a siren of the damned.

Kore hovered above her, arms outstretched—glowing, magnificent, monstrous.

"Now you'll know what it feels like," she said, voice trembling with venom. "To be seen not as a sister… not as a daughter… but as a *thing*. A cursed thing. A threat to be caged. A nightmare to be buried."

The chains hissed, burning into Edith's skin.

This was her penance.

This was the price of mercy.

Because in that moment, Edith knew with crushing clarity:

Compassion had failed her.

And love…

Love had unleashed a cataclysm.

Epilogue

Edith's head snapped upward, breath hitching, chains rattling softly like distant funeral bells. The effort alone sent needles of agony through her shoulders and spine—her wings long since torn and cauterized, her veins drained of anything divine. The light in her blood had dulled to an ember.

She did not dare move again.

She'd learned that lesson early.

Every twitch of defiance triggered the chains—surgical in design, parasitic in purpose. The cuffs embedded in her limbs weren't just restraints—they were siphons, leeching her power molecule by molecule. What little strength remained was just enough to breathe, and even that came with a price. The table beneath her was cold steel, the surface slick with blood—her blood—dried into constellations of failure.

Weeks. Or maybe longer.

Time meant nothing in this white-lit tomb.

Around her, figures passed in silence. Scientists cloaked in pale coats, the bold black letters *W.A.S.P.* emblazoned across their backs like warnings. They treated her not as a prisoner, nor even as a weapon—but as a specimen. A dismantled god, dissected in increments.

They never spoke to her. Only about her.

"Cellular decay still slowing..."

"Residual aura scans remain inconclusive..."

"Get the injector. She moved again."

Then came the sound.

Boom.

A deep, echoing rupture. Not like the humming sterilized doors or the mechanical whir of equipment. No—this was chaos. A surge of feral combat. Something was tearing its way through the facility.

Gunfire.

Screams.

The sound of bodies hitting walls. Flesh on tile.

Glass shattering in succession like breaking hymns.

Edith's pulse quickened.

Kore? No.

This wasn't her sister. This energy... it was similar. But not born of hate. Not divine, either. It was other. Familiar and alien all at once, like a half-forgotten nightmare clawing its way back into waking memory.

The lab doors hissed.

From the smoke-steeped hall beyond, a figure emerged.

He didn't walk. He stalked—casually, confidently, as if the world itself bent around his stride. Clad in a tailored black-and-red suit that clung like living skin, the man looked like a devil drawn from memory. Red tendrils of lightning danced across his shoulders, snapping softly in the fluorescent light. His hair was blood-silk and fell to his chest in perfect sheets. His eyes, unreadable, shimmered with a crimson sheen.

A flask clinked softly in his hand.

He took a swig. Unbothered. Unhurried.

Gunfire still echoed behind him like applause.

Edith blinked hard, struggling to focus through the fevered haze. "Who the hell are you?"

The man looked at her—through her. And he smiled. Not kindly. Not cruelly. But knowingly. A man who'd seen extinction and smiled back.

She frowned, her throat raw. "You're not with them?"

He laughed. Short. Sharp. Like thunder clipped into a whisper. "Does it look like I wear name tags?"

Another scream tore from somewhere down the hall. A gurgled cry. Then silence.

He stepped closer, lightning rippling through the air with every footfall. Instruments around him shorted and died.

"The world's gone to shit, sweetheart," he said, looking down at her restraints. "Move your ass, or stay chained up and die. I don't give a fuck."

His hand hovered over the chains. The metal hissed, recoiled—afraid.

She tried again, her voice more blood than breath. "Who *are* you?"

He didn't answer.

He didn't have to.

With a flash of red light, the chains shattered.

About the Author

W.W. Mitchell is a versatile storyteller who never shies away from pushing the limits of his imagination. His works span a wide range of genres, from gritty, raw narratives to inspiring tales, all of which immerse readers in vivid, otherworldly experiences. Whether exploring distant galaxies, unraveling deep mysteries, or examining the complexities of human nature, Mitchell's stories always transport readers to uncharted realms.

Born in Newark, New Jersey, and raised in Orlando, Florida, Mitchell's early life was shaped by his love of storytelling and the diverse influences of his surroundings. After graduating, he made the bold decision to enlist in the United States Marine Corps, embarking on a journey that took him across the globe. His experiences in the military, particularly those spent navigating unfamiliar lands and cultures, profoundly shaped his narrative voice, giving his work a unique, grounded perspective.

Throughout his military service, Mitchell developed a deep appreciation for discipline, resilience, and the human spirit, themes that often weave their way into his writing. But it wasn't just the world of war that influenced him—it was the stories he encountered along the way, whether from his fellow Marines or the people he met in far-flung corners of the Earth. These experiences fostered his passion for storytelling and sparked his desire to craft stories that resonate on both an emotional and intellectual level.

Eager to expand his creative horizons, Mitchell later turned to screenwriting, adding a new dimension to his narrative skill set. This expansion allowed him to explore his characters in new ways and experiment with cinematic elements that have since become hallmarks of his work. His multifaceted approach to storytelling, combining elements of literature and film, ensures that each of his stories is as dynamic and visually captivating as it is emotionally engaging.

Today, W.W. Mitchell continues to weave together complex, multifaceted stories that challenge the imagination and invite readers to journey beyond the ordinary. His passion for storytelling, combined with his diverse experiences, makes him a distinctive voice in the world of fiction, one that promises to keep readers on the edge of their seats, eager to discover what comes next.

You can connect with me on:

🌐 https://www.w-w-m.com

🐦 https://x.com/weasmitchell

f　　https://www.facebook.com/profile.php?id=61556323875593

🔗 https://www.trigonicmedia.com

Also by W.W. Mitchell

The journey after Cataclysm Kin CONTINUES!

Going Rogue

"The possession grew stronger, and pain became an inconsequential sensation. I perceived every movement around me with uncanny ease, anticipating actions before they unfolded. In a swift and fluid motion, as my assailant blinked, I redirected his arm, seized the blade, and drove it into his neck. Blood erupted, painting the night with steel and crimson as he collapsed, gasping for air.

Lifting his writhing form, I slammed him onto the unforgiving concrete, witnessing the shattering of bone and the gush of blood from his neck. A dark stain marked the pavement, and something inside me pushed a moan from my throat, satiating a primal thirst for violence with actions beyond my conscious control."

Unleash The Fire Within

In the heart-pounding science fiction thriller "Going Rogue," readers are taken on a captivating journey alongside Malacai Rogue, a former convict whose life is forever changed by a cosmic event.

After being struck by lightning, Malacai finds himself sharing his body with an otherworldly being,
granting him incredible power and knowledge.
However, Malacai's life takes a dangerous turn
when he is captured by a mysterious organization
with hidden agendas and vast resources. Tasked
with preventing the activation of a devastating
superweapon, Malacai is forced into a high-stakes
partnership. As Malacai navigates a web of deception and suspense, he must confront his inner
demons while dealing with the alien entity now
residing within him. Teaming up with a daring operative who offers him a substantial sum of money,
Malacai embarks on a perilous journey across the
globe and through enemy territory. With time
running out and the fate of the world at stake,
Malacai must fully embrace his newfound abilities,
face his past, and form unexpected alliances. In a
race against time and seemingly insurmountable
odds, Malacai Rogue embodies the perfect blend
of human strength and extraterrestrial power in a
battle to save not only his world, but the entire
universe from destruction. "Going Rogue" is a
gripping tale of redemption, sacrifice, and the
unwavering determination of a man thrust into
a destiny beyond his imagination. Filled with
unexpected twists and suspenseful moments, this
thrilling story delves into the essence of heroism,

the cost of freedom, and the strength of unity when faced with threats from the unknown reaches of the cosmos.